Edited by Colin Amery

The National Theatre: 'The Architectural Review' Guide

The Architectural Press Ltd : London

Contents

'*Going round by way of Lambeth one afternoon in the early summer of 1870, we had skirted the Thames along the Surrey bank, crossed the river higher up, and on our way back were returning at our leisure through Westminster; when, just as we were approaching the shadow of the old Abbey at Poet's Corner, under the roof-beams of which he was so soon to be laid in his grave, with a rain of tears and flowers, he abruptly asked—"What do you think would be the realisation of one of my most cherished day-dreams?"*

Adding, instantly, without waiting for any answer, "To settle down now for the remainder of my life within easy distance of a great theatre, in the direction of which I should hold supreme authority. It should be a house, of course, having a skilled and noble company, and one in every way magnificently appointed. The pieces acted should be dealt with according to my pleasure, and touched up here and there in obedience to my own judgment; the players as well as the plays being absolutely under my command. There," said he,

laughingly, and in a glow at the mere fancy, "that's my day dream."

The day dreamer on the South Bank was Charles Dickens. He was sceptical about the foundation of a National Theatre and his doubts have been justified by the long years of debate and delay that have preceded the creation of the new theatre. Further on in this issue Iain Mackintosh looks back at the chequered careers of the buildings that until 1976 have been our surrogate national theatres.

Mark Girouard

Facing page: an audience gathers in the Olivier Theatre, where the architectural drama reaches its climax under this majestical roof. In the article below Mark Girouard describes the impression the architecture makes on a visitor to the theatre.

Cosmic connections

It is a curious experience to sit in the upper tiers of the Olivier while a play is on. One feels at the centre of more than the National Theatre. It is as though the theatre were a burning glass, through which sections of the world were being concentrated on to the circle of light above which one is suspended. One is in a dark cave or shell, focusing on the action which is taking place in it, yet at the same time aware of the outside world, endless and teeming. The stage is the centre of a web, drawing its actors in along five lines which stretch (or seem to stretch) outside the theatre: three lines vanish into the seemingly limitless backstage, two lines tunnel under the auditorium. And the shell under which one is sitting is a shattered shell; the cave has gaps in it. The balance between feeling shut in, and yet not shut in, is exciting and also very skilful. There is a sense of immensity on tap, yet none of rattling round in an immense space; the scale is human.

Two devices, of colour and form, help produce the effect of an enclosure which does not completely enclose. When the lights are down, the black-painted side walls act, in effect, as a void in contrast to the enclosing structure of the white concrete. And the shell is literally cracked apart overhead and shattered into many fragments at the back of the auditorium. This cracking and shattering is used for purposes of stage lighting and acoustics, but its effect is also visual and symbolic. It suggests an aesthetic of broken forms which is taken up by the jaggedly broken concrete walls of the side tiers, running down to the stage to end in beaked prows curving round it.

During any play one is aware, from time to time, of the audience watching the play, as well as of the play itself. It is not a distraction because the people in the audience are part of the drama; the play succeeds in so far as it reflects (or challenges) their own experience or desires, and their absorption adds to its intensity. So the disposition of the audience is important; it can be arranged boringly or excitingly. The audience at the Olivier, terraced, tiered, lifted up in the prows to either side of the stage, and dimly seen against the blackness, is visually an exciting one. There is something of the same effect during a performance in the Lyttelton, where the white concrete galleries standing out against the black surround set off the audience—especially the side galleries, striated and

piled up like miniature Mappin terraces, with a frieze of watching faces along their crest.

But the Lyttelton is deliberately a more conventional (and, presumably not deliberately, a less comfortable) theatre than the Olivier; it has none of its magic, none of that vivid feeling of being at the centre of things. The Olivier is cosmic. This is not a pretentious adjective, but a descriptive one. The Olivier was designed under the influence not only of individual theatres from Epidaurus to the Globe, but of Classical and Renaissance theories of the theatre as a microcosm, a little model of the world connected by its architecture to something bigger than itself. There are Classical and Renaissance echoes in the five entrances to the stage, the shape of the auditorium, and the upper-level gallery behind the stage, which has already been put to brilliant use in *Tamburlaine*. More generally, the Olivier sets out to be a *theatrum mundi, theatrum orbis, theatrum vitae humanae* in the sense rediscovered for this generation by Frances Yates, of whom Lasdun is an admirer. It sets out and it succeeds; and in doing so it puts an instrument of exciting power into the hands of the producer. It is an instrument which should have range as well as power; there seems no reason why the burning-glass circle should not concentrate as effectively on the personal drama of two or three people as the global exploits of Tamburlaine.

During the play the audience is only a subsidiary part of the drama. At the National Theatre it, and oneself in it, comes into its own in the intervals. It then becomes the play, and each member of it is at once actor and spectator. One parades up and down through a series of inter-connecting stage sets, striking conscious or unconscious attitudes and watching others do the same. One looks up at people leaning over balconies above one, or down through clefts, along valleys, or into pits, at the people parading below. One samples the sideshows provided. If wise, one heads for the Olivier bars when at the Lyttelton and the Lyttelton bars when at the Olivier. Once again the action takes place in a cave, or series of caves, and once again there are holes in it. But this time, instead of sensing the world outside, it is possible to look through the gaps and see it—and (in summer) to walk out on to the balconies and see it even closer. The views change in scope and size as one walks round, from arrow-slit vignettes of parked cars in distorted perspective to full spreads of Somerset House, lit up across the darkly gleaming river. The combination of stage sets within and backcloths without induces a sense of agreeable unreality; the chance sight of the two occupants of the box office locked in a clinch together seems all part of the fun. If one had nothing else to thank the National Theatre for, one would bless it for making intervals enjoyable. Good-bye to fights for drinks in hot little rooms, as though at an especially unpleasant cocktail party, at which one knows, and wants to know, nobody. Good-bye to the quick dash through the rain to the nearest pub, the whisky knocked down too fast, and the quick dash back again. Or for those who can face neither of these alternatives, good-bye to aimless standing in draughty foyers, or ice creams in empty auditoria, with nothing to do but thumb through the programme and stare at the safety curtain.

Most theatre-goers can abandon themselves just to enjoying the foyers at the National, but anyone interested in architecture will try to analyse how they work. The basic geography is that the Olivier is on a higher level than the Lyttelton, and that the axes of the two theatres are set at 45 degrees to each other. The basic units are the four concrete trays that mark each level, inside and out, the board-shaped concrete columns that support the trays, and the staircases that join them. The basic materials are carpeting, glass and concrete, the latter coffered in the trays and board-marked in the walls; at night the board-marking is lit in relief by lights set in the floor, so that the concrete acquires a texture that looks something between canvas and fur, and is caressing rather than cold. The basic strategy is to join layer to layer, and space to space, not just by breaking through the trays, but also by constantly making small apertures through other elements, to give unexpected views into the adjacent spaces. The mesh which provides a basic discipline is an overlay of two grids based on the axes of the two theatres, with the Lyttelton grid on the main, and the Olivier grid on the secondary one. The Olivier grid fixes features such as the lift towers and the coffering of the trays, which as a result is usually at 45 degrees to the perimeters of the trays themselves. The grids superimposed produce the main staircases, with their half-hexagon landings split open at the centre to give views through, to distant figures down below or up above. The repertory is not especially large (there are other

elements, but these are the main ones) and few if any of the motifs or devices in it are new; they are drawn from the vocabulary of the Modern Movement. But when used together they allow for endless different combinations, and the sum total is like nothing else, a rich, complex, at times mysterious, sometimes confusing but almost always enjoyable sequence of spaces, where columns of delicious slenderness can soar through several storeys of open space, or transfix staircases like skewers, where climbing each flight of stairs reveals a new vista and the space of every vista vanishes enticingly out of sight round a corner.

'Only connect': the theme of E. M. Forster's *Howard's End* could be the motto of the National Theatre. The stage of the Olivier sticks its prongs into the outside world, the different levels of the different foyers are not only shot through with connections internally, but link with the city outside. At three separate levels one can walk out of the theatre, not just on to the exterior balconies but into London, on to or under Waterloo bridge, or on to the river terraces. Or one can drive into the car parks underneath it, which are as depressing as any underground car parks; but at least, once through the swing doors, one goes straight at basement level into the shapely and mysterious world of the foyers. The foyers, and the bars, restaurants, shows and activities in them, are open to anyone from morning till night.

Only connect—the ambitions and possibilities of the National Theatre are so great that one finds oneself anxiously totting up the occasions on which the connections fail to work. There are aspects which it is too early yet to judge because they are still in an incomplete stage—notably the stage machinery, the lighting and the acoustics. To judge from the inadequate experience of one performance of *Tamburlaine*, there is an element of censorship in the Olivier acoustics which is all to the good —clear, simple diction comes across clearly and simply, ranting and what might be called the Shakespeare voice (which one knows is Shakespeare the moment one turns on the Third Programme) vanishes through the top of the theatre. Yet one is left with an element of doubt which won't be resolved until final adjustments have been made, and actors have learnt the feel of the theatre.

Outside the auditoria, connections occasionally break

down. The back of the theatre, however sensible as a screen wall for workshops, presents a face of unwelcoming blankness to the outside world. The middle level of the Lyttelton foyer is at its worst in the daytime, when the balustrade of the approach playform outside uncomfortably blocks the windows and the view, and the concrete coffering seems oppressively low; at night, lighting inside and darkness out changes the emphasis and the proportions. One expects the upper levels of the Lyttelton foyer to join up with the Olivier foyer, but they don't, and a circular staircase which looks as though it is going to join them fails to make the connection. From the lower level, or looking down from Waterloo bridge, the approach road and river terrace seem to impose an unnecessarily large barrier between the theatre and the water. Inevitably, one finds oneself wondering why the theatre was not built dramatically on top of the river. Second thoughts make it clear that, apart from what the GLC may or may not have allowed, there was also a design decision here; if the theatre had been closer to the river, the balconies would have shut out the view of the water from the foyers. A theatre over the river might have been exciting, but it would have had to be a different kind of building.

Only connect—the biggest obstacle to connection, in the daytime especially, is the neighbourhood. In the days of the Globe the South Bank was the Elizabethan equivalent of Shaftesbury Avenue or Leicester Square. The National Theatre, if dropped into Leicester Square, would be immediately life-enhancing, because the life is there to be enhanced; as it is, unless its own food, drink and entertainment are really good and competitive (75p for a sandwich is not good enough) and unless something lively and sympathetic goes up on the empty plot to the north and the moribund plot to the east, it runs the risk of catching the neighbourhood blight instead of dispersing it.

But regardless of what goes on inside it, the National Theatre also exists as an object, a new and prominent addition to the townscape, whether seen from the bridge or the streets or, best of all perhaps, from across the river. What one sees is complex, striated, many featured, but, as an image, basically simple: the strata rise up through subsidiary peaks to the dominating peak of the Olivier fly tower. Regarded simply as a piece of abstract sculpture

it is infinitely more accomplished than the neighbouring Hayward; the latter now looks like a hanger-on, getting his master into disrepute by imitating his worst mannerisms. But one must at least be grateful to the Hayward for framing one of the best views of the National through its upper level window. From this, on a dry sunny day, the Alpine landscape of snowy peaks gradually rising and retreating is an amazing and exciting sight. But on a wet day the National looks dark and sombre, unlike its opposite across the river, Somerset House, the Portland stone of which is gay and festive whatever the weather. The theatre, though not inimical to gaiety going on inside it, could never be described as either gay or festive in its architecture. It is a serious building, the product of a movement which is basically serious, not to say puritanical. Because of this it is unlikely, as a landmark, to inspire immediate affection; it is a smoulderer, not a fizzer.

London has acquired few large public, as opposed to commercial, buildings since the war; apart from the National Theatre what is there except Euston Station, London Airport, and the South Bank complex? And who likes or admires any of these except the Festival Hall? To have launched a building as momentous as the National Theatre should have cheered us up, in a period of national blues. Instead we are told that we can't afford it, don't need it, and that Peter Hall is impossible anyway. These reactions, at first so depressingly suggestive of total loss of nerve, are, in fact, the routine ones that greet all new national landmarks. They almost inevitably cost more and take longer to build than they were meant to, offend numerous vested interests, and are stylistically out of fashion by the time they are finished. Wren was sacked before St Paul's was completed, and smart young Palladians thought its architecture a disgrace to the metropolis.The building of the Houses of Parliament was punctuated by interminable rows, mainly because it cost too much and because the expensively up-to-date ventilation system never worked; well before it was finished its Perpendicular Gothic styling was considered effeminate and hopelessly out of date. The Law Courts had such a rough passage that they killed poor George Edmund Street. Like them, the National Theatre can afford to wait.

William Curtis

Past and prejudice

It will probably be years before a clear historical view of the National Theatre becomes possible. Surprisingly little fact has emerged concerning the social forces which created it and the design process which led to its final form.

This is not odd given the recentness of the building's completion, but the picture does seem to be more blurred than usual for a new arrival. Perhaps this is because the theatre collides with some of the dearest of contemporary prejudices. The theatre is a monument and at present monuments are regarded with suspicion in England—as if they were dinosaurs from a previous age or the products of *prima donnas* intent on self-aggrandisement. Monuments, it is intimated, are not what modern architecture (or post-modern architecture depending where you stand) is about.

This leads to the next prejudice, which concerns size, sculptural quality and materials. The National Theatre is big, forceful and made of concrete when the prevalent ethos requires the petite, the anonymous and the vernacular, no matter what the building task.

The theatre has its roots in the international modern movement and the idealism which guided that movement but there has been a general and probably understandable loss of faith in this tradition.

The theatre confidently concerns itself with questions of form but the last thing a crisis- and conscience-stricken architectural profession wishes to discuss is the problem of form in architecture. Aesthetics go to the bottom of the list while morality, sociology and politics go to the top.

Finally the theatre, which was launched in the economic conditions of the early 1960s, arrives in the midst of a slump. In the circumstances it seems natural that factions should exist who ask if this is not cake when bread is what is needed. It is part of the present cultural transition that professionalism is held suspect: as a creation of professionals the theatre provides an affront to populists of every stripe. Had the theatre opened five years ago, it would have encountered a different set of prejudices for and against it; and in five years' time, it will meet another set. For the moment it is clear that the theatre does not accommodate itself readily to the fashions and prejudices of the latter half of 1976.

Even if the theatre were fashionable, it would not make a fair historical assessment of the building easier: it is difficult to write the history of the very recent past. But one may pose the basic historical questions knowing full well that the answers are bound to be incomplete. How and why did the building come out in its present form? What ideas lie behind it? How does it fit into the architect's *oeuvre*? How does it relate to the history of architecture and the history of theatre design? What are its apparent strengths and weaknesses? These are some of the questions which would have to be considered by a historian working at any time. But one must begin with the thing itself.

Facing page: layer upon layer of geometry makes a strange and moving setting for interior drama.

'We have tried to offset the current scepticism about the permanent housing of institutionalised culture and the doubts about architectural form-making by a response away from the isolated monument and towards an architecture of urban landscape. It is an architecture without facades but with layers of building, like geological strata, connected in such a way that they flow into the surrounding riverscape and city. The building is thus an extension of the theatre into the everyday world from which it springs. The strata inside and outside are the basic vocabulary. They seem to capture the fundamental sense of theatre as a place of gathering and they provide a framework for the experience of visiting the theatre which takes the city itself as its backdrop.'

D.L.

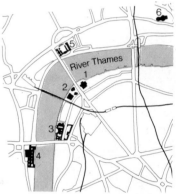

location plan

key
1, National Theatre
2, Festival Hall, Queen Elizabeth Hall, Hayward Gallery
3, County Hall
4, Houses of Parliament
5, Somerset House
6, St Paul's

Top: the National Theatre is unquestionably a landmark, it joins the Barbican towers (left) and the Queen Elizabeth Hall (right) as a solid, indestructible example of mid-twentieth-century design.
Far left: from the river the clear geometry rises above the terraces, the fly towers of the Olivier (left) and the Lyttelton (right) signal the stages at the heart of the building.
Left: the high tower of the Olivier Theatre broods over the entire South Bank; it is like a white mountain in the sun but has a sombre inscrutability in grey London weather.

Facing page: night brings the building to life, skilfully lit layers of dense honeycomb lure the audience inside.
Left: the visual language of the building is composed of a calm arrangement of simple elements: angled towers, a diagonal grid and long, level terraces.

The great experiment

Laurence Olivier (former director of the National Theatre) talks to Colin Amery

The National Theatre Company was founded in 1962 with Laurence Olivier as director. It played at Chichester and the Old Vic and Olivier was very involved in the long and complicated debate about the nature of a National Theatre building. For many years before 1962 Olivier had been a trustee of the Shakespeare Memorial National Theatre Committee, he joined this group of 'very grey-headed gentlemen' to ensure that a representative building committee would be created.

LORD OLIVIER: *I told them I wouldn't be interested in a National Theatre without a proper building committee. At that time there were only two actors in the group, John Geilgud and me, and the director Norman Marshall—there was not one theatre designer. The designer is the man who really ought to be consulted, all his life he has been tortured by the shape of the stage, the relationship to the audience and whether or not the proscenium should remain.*

CA: During all the discussions about the final shape of the Olivier theatre did you find yourself sorting out in your own mind the pros and cons of the proscenium theatre?

LORD OLIVIER: *Well, after Lasdun had made it clear that we couldn't have an adaptable theatre of any great size I found that I was imagining a theatre that was almost arena-like in shape. I worked at Chichester in order to discover how well the open stage worked. I secretly had my tongue in my cheek about it because I always felt that the open stage boys had gone back in time. Shakespeare had that sort of theatre. I suppose that the actors evolved the proscenium, the chap playing Richard III said, 'Let's go back a bit further then I'll only have to look in one direction when I'm making an aside'. And then the comedian said, 'It's awful to say one thing and get a laugh from this side and not the other because they can't see the face I'm pulling'. And bit by bit they went back and the proscenium was evolved. It arrived soon after Shakespeare's time and I always rather laughingly supposed that it must have seemed a tremendous improvement in their minds or they wouldn't have done it Now we see the open stage as a great step forward—it is and it isn't.*
I recently opened the Royal Exchange Theatre in Manchester which is as good a theatre completely in the round as you could find. There is something about having the play right amongst you that is very good. I had to make a speech and for a single performer it is almost impossible to cope with a full circle.

CA: But when you are directing a play for the open stage or in the round, don't you feel it is the grouping of the actors that counts? Some of the audience may only see the back of the actor's head but then they can see the expressions of the audience opposite—you get a different sort of vibrancy in the theatre.

LORD OLIVIER: *You certainly get different scenes with different dynamics, the point of Chichester emerged during the first season. For a very popular play like 'Uncle Vanya' the audience would say, 'I want to sit here tonight. I want to be near the scene between Miss Plowright and Sybil Thorndike at the end of the row scene, when they have their dialogue together.' People used to come two or three times and sit in*

15

(succeeded by Sound Research Laboratories).
Graphic design: Ken Briggs.
Catering: Greene Bertram Smith & Company.

The National Theatre Building Committee
Lord Olivier, Norman Marshall (joint chairmen); Stephen Arlen, Michael Benthall, Peter Brook, George Devine, John Dexter, Frank Dunlop, Michael Elliott, Roger Furse, William Gaskill, Peter Hall, Jocelyn Herbert, Sean Kenny, Tanya Moiseiwitsch, Richard Pilbrow, Michel St Denis, Robert Stephens. (Kenneth Tynan was also consulted.)

Main contractor
Sir Robert McAlpine and Sons Ltd.

Description
The National Theatre stands a little downstream of Waterloo Bridge on the South Bank of the Thames where the river begins to turn into Kings Reach and to sweep around towards the City. Two blank fly towers rise from layers of horizontal terraces. These are inhabited on many levels. They cascade to the riverside walk and create deep undercrofts, shadows and recesses. The concrete is whitish-grey, bare and unadorned. Its planes and facets hover out towards the surroundings

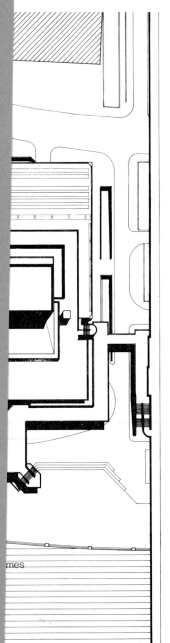

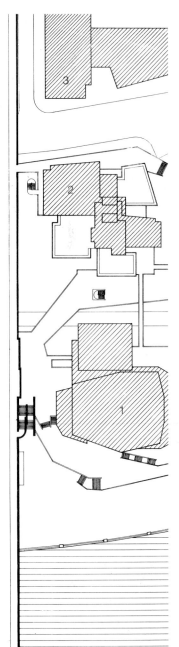

Waterloo Bridge

17

and are modelled in light.

The terraces are clearly a primary feature. They bind the building into a coherent whole and extend back and forth in response to changes of function, interior space and exterior possibility of view. They support the public life of the structure and open out its contents to the cityscape, as well as supporting the major functions inside.

The towers are the vertical accompaniment to the terraces. They house flying equipment, elevators and ventilating machinery. Of various sizes, they also indicate the presence of the theatres within and the position of the main entrance along the 45-degree axis to the open theatre stage.

The open stage (Olivier) theatre occupies a large area away from the bridge.

The proscenium (Lyttelton) theatre is considerably smaller, so that in plan, the

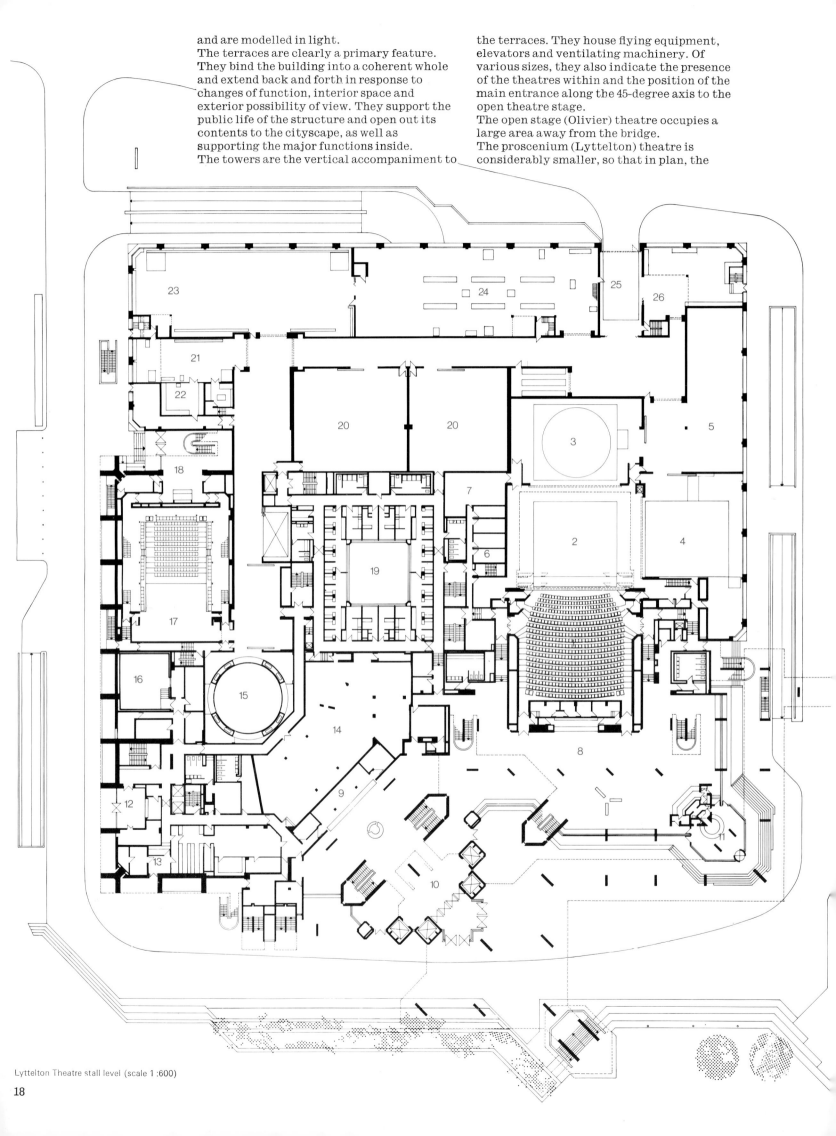

Lyttelton Theatre stall level (scale 1:600)

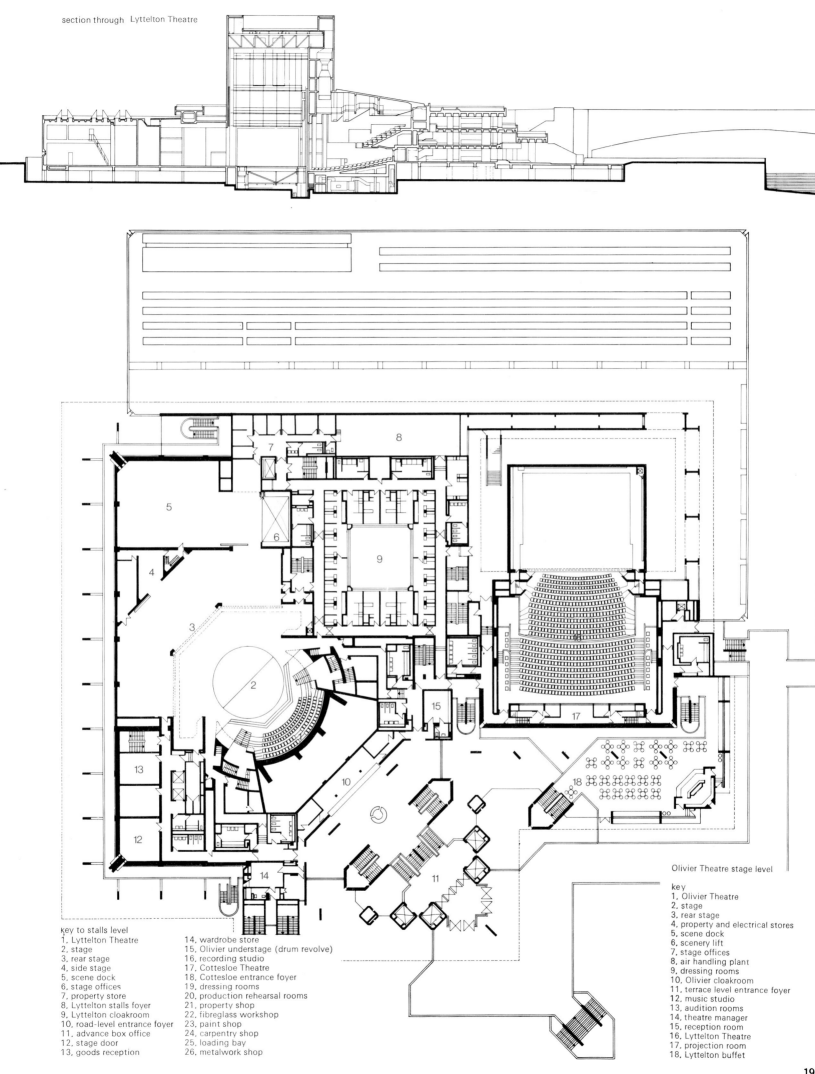

section through Lyttelton Theatre

key to stalls level
1. Lyttelton Theatre
2. stage
3. rear stage
4. side stage
5. scene dock
6. stage offices
7. property store
8. Lyttelton stalls foyer
9. Lyttelton cloakroom
10. road-level entrance foyer
11. advance box office
12. stage door
13. goods reception
14. wardrobe store
15. Olivier understage (drum revolve)
16. recording studio
17. Cottesloe Theatre
18. Cottesloe entrance foyer
19. dressing rooms
20. production rehearsal rooms
21. property shop
22. fibreglass workshop
23. paint shop
24. carpentry shop
25. loading bay
26. metalwork shop

Olivier Theatre stage level

key
1. Olivier Theatre
2. stage
3. rear stage
4. property and electrical stores
5. scene dock
6. scenery lift
7. stage offices
8. air handling plant
9. dressing rooms
10. Olivier cloakroom
11. terrace level entrance foyer
12. music studio
13. audition rooms
14. theatre manager
15. reception room
16. Lyttelton Theatre
17. projection room
18. Lyttelton buffet

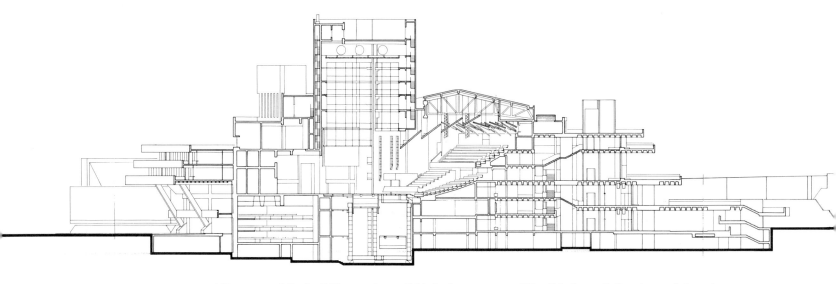

section through Olivier Theatre

public zones of the building make an L linked by the receding terraces. They are set back surprisingly far from the river bank. All these ceremonial parts are made from *in-situ* concrete. To the rear is a more neutral brick and concrete box containing the 'private' areas—paint shops, workrooms and rehearsal spaces. The third small theatre and dressing rooms are tucked in between the two main zones.

That the open theatre is the prime mover of the design is clear from the exterior and from the plan. Form, structure and circulation converge on it and the auditorium is itself

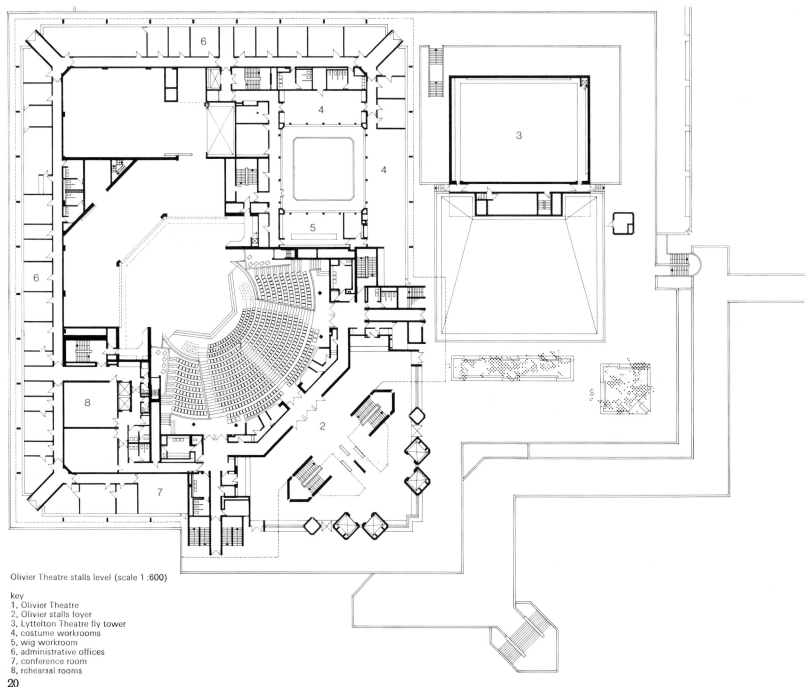

Olivier Theatre stalls level (scale 1 :600)

key
1. Olivier Theatre
2. Olivier stalls foyer
3. Lyttelton Theatre fly tower
4. costume workrooms
5. wig workroom
6. administrative offices
7. conference room
8. rehearsal rooms

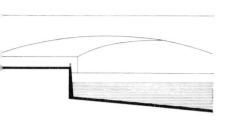

highly focused. The axis of the open theatre sets up a 45-degree angle which is repeated in many parts and details of the building. All elements of the design respond to one or other of the main directions of the auditoria. The spatial layering observed on the exterior is also felt on the interior. Banks of stairs pass to the upper floors. Volumes open up as many as three levels at a time. The concrete skeleton—a constituent feature of much modern architecture—has here sidestepped its usual grid and box formula. Instead one finds rich sequences of form and space, flowing into each other, opening to admit more light, or closing to give a sense of protection. Elements shift and align in new relationships as one moves about the interiors. The magic of the river and the city is experienced as a series of scenographic vignettes framed by the overhanging soffits of the ceiling. The details of the theatre are everywhere integrated with the primary forms. The raking struts supporting the north-east corner are a case in point—not only do they serve their structural function, they have also been delicately scaled so that from across the river they have a springing, vital visual effect,

like inverted flying buttresses. Formwork has been designed to echo major directions of larger elements, and fenestration joints have been made to insure an easy visual transition from inside to out. The platforms and terraces join with the stalls and upper tier levels of the main auditoria and give access to them from the rear. The bare concrete, banked seats and horizontal tiers in the Olivier Theatre continue the theme of stratification observed in the building. The auditorium is arranged in a 90-degree arc which appears to grasp the circular stage and hence to unify the world of the audience with that of the actor. The sense of focus is enhanced by a fairly steep rake and the angle of the side walls. Side banks of seats stand at a transitional level between stalls and upper tier and, as well as further emphasising the sense of convergence, these help to unify the entire auditorium—there is a sense of continuity between stalls and upper tier which is rare. The acoustic ceiling is raked as a concave echo of the bowl of seats beneath it. Certain properties of the design are immediately evident. The furthest seat is 70ft from the stage and this allows for considerable

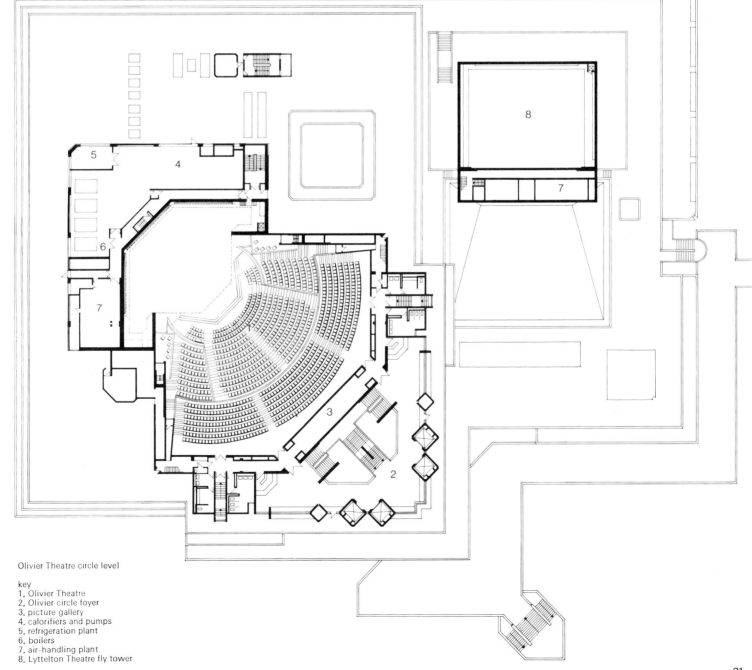

Olivier Theatre circle level

key
1. Olivier Theatre
2. Olivier circle foyer
3. picture gallery
4. calorifiers and pumps
5. refrigeration plant
6. boilers
7. air-handling plant
8. Lyttelton Theatre fly tower

intimacy between audience and actor. The arc is limited to 130 degrees so that the actor can 'control' the whole span of his audience when confronting the central axis. A few rows of 'ripple' seats are set just below the stage: these have an important psychological function as they help the actor to transmit nuances to the audience.

The Lyttelton Theatre is a highly efficient proscenium theatre with an upper tier, slightly curved seats and bare concrete walls. The proscenium wall is adjustable so that the character of the theatre varies from a species of end stage to a complete separation of the actor's world from audience's by means of a picture frame.

The studio theatre is to the east end of the theatre on the side furthest from Waterloo Bridge. In contrast to the main auditoria, it is a room with completely flexible seating arrangements. The offices, canteen and administrative functions of the theatre are concentrated along this side of the building too, and those near the north-east corner of the structure afford views towards St Paul's.

Above: the interior street backstage.
Above right: a dressing room cubicle.
Right: costume workroom.
Facing page: cut-away axonometric by Tony Dyson showing the foyer spaces.

Dressing rooms are placed between and behind the main stages and are lit by a courtyard cut through the strata at that point. The character of these spaces is straightforward—a simple warehouse aesthetic.

The same can be said of the maze of supporting functions to the rear, though these are of a size which can happily cope with large scenery and scenery trucks. Finishes are bare brick or concrete and the structure is exhibited frankly. Paint shops, rehearsal rooms and a veritable factory for producing props of all kinds give on to a giant interior street which in turn gives access to the rear of the stages.

Criticism

William Curtis assesses the National Theatre (his detailed historical analysis is on pp52-58)

Whether one thinks a building successful or not must depend ultimately on what one thinks architecture should be doing. There is little consensus on this at present beyond weakly disguised revisions of 'firmness, commodity and delight'. As was suggested in the introduction, the prevalent emphasis in England seems to be on 'commodity'. There is certainly little emphasis on or agreement about 'delight'—or what is beautiful. There is not even shared opinion about *what* buildings should look like for there is no common architectural language.

Still some attempt at judging the National Theatre must be made in terms of function, social values, siting, form and symbolism. Criticism must emanate from consideration of the problems facing the architects and from some sense of how things might have been done differently.

It would be silly to judge whether or not the theatre will 'work' after only a few months' use of its auditoria. Still, some strengths and weaknesses can be highlighted. The chief point of going to the theatre is to enjoy a play. This requires an environment which offers the maximum comfort and convenience and the minimum interference with the 'sacred' relationship—that between audience and actor. Ideally this minimum definition will be enriched by a beautiful setting to enhance the drama and what comes before and after it.

On most of these points the National Theatre must surely be rated a success. The painstaking care which went into the design of the main auditoria seems to have paid off. Acoustics and visibility are of high quality. Seats are comfortable, well spaced and easy of access. Quality of light and air is impeccable. Gangways are sufficiently wide to avoid cramming in intervals and at the end of a play. The relationship between audience and actor is unobstructed and, in the Olivier Theatre particularly, it is enhanced by spatial order of the room described earlier. The character of the Lyttelton lacks this spatial charge, but it cannot be described as a prosaic setting. Large crowds disperse rapidly into separate groups at intervals but without loss of concentration and without loss of that sense—strongly felt in the Olivier—of being involved in a shared event. That the concrete finish will trigger many of the usual reactions is to be expected, given standard expectations of stucco, mirrors and red velvet—and this despite the fact that the concrete has been superbly finished throughout, well matched with other materials and is in any case the source of the building's spatial and contextual richness. The majority seem to react favourably to the scale, vistas and intimacy of the great foyers.

Similar ambivalence is likely in the reaction of the public to the theatre's exteriors. On the positive side there may be enjoyment of the life on the terraces and of the river below; perhaps too, some will appreciate the building's fine proportions, spaces and sequences. On the negative side there may be instinctive dislike of concrete and of large

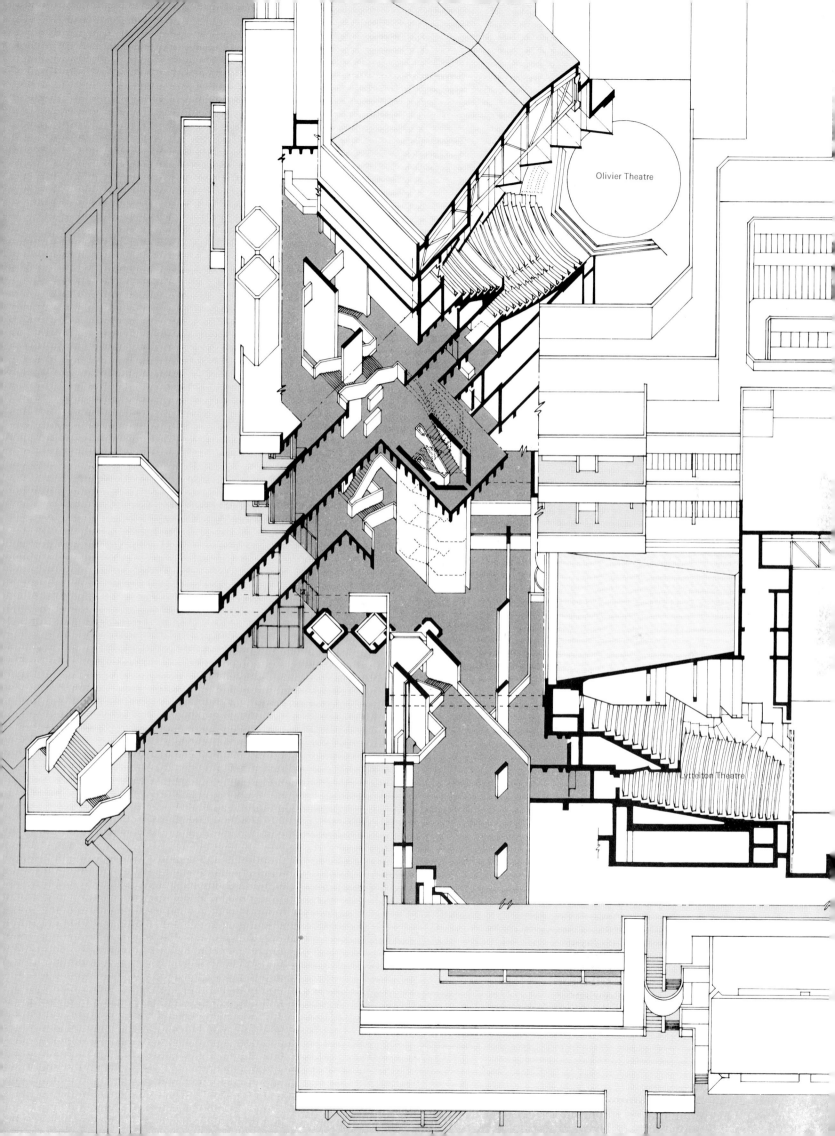

Olivier Theatre

Lyttelton Theatre

Blank rear view of the theatre.

areas of greyness relatively unmodified by other colours. Perhaps too, there will be some carping at the distance of the entrances from the bridge. There is a real issue here, for despite their hospitable symbolic stance to the city as a whole, the strata are hard to penetrate just by the bridge.

The urban landscape idea of the building is at its best on the river side. The east side with its raking buttresses is forbidding in scale. The west side is fine where the strata meet the bridge, but further back it becomes really problematic where the brick and concrete box containing the workshops, etc presents an almost unbroken, sheer face to the passerby. This sense of exclusion reaches a climax to the rear. Many forces in the design have led to this result: the workshops clearly belong to the rear; the design as a whole insists on a distinction between public and private and one certainly would not expect the workshops to be opened up to the surroundings, for the area to the rear encourages little friendliness being, at the moment, dead; the building requires a visual base, long and horizontal, at this point. Even so, one senses that the theatre might have given some hint as to the direction this part of the city might have taken. Instead, it presents a blank.

Perhaps the problem of the blank back part of the building points to an unresolved issue in Lasdun's system. The arrangement of sheer facades and large overhangs lacking the strata scale occurs in both Christ's College at Cambridge and the University of London schemes. Both present inhospitable proportions to their (admittedly unexceptional) rear access streets. On the other hand it seems that the architect is deliberately working to separate the pedestrian precincts and walkways created by the strata from the motor vehicle which passes behind or beneath: an urbanistic principle is being demonstrated vigorously with perhaps some loss of attention to particular demands in each building task. Something of this problem emerges too in the dressing room and office zones where the strata provide an order which is almost too controlling.

The pay-off on the river side of the theatre is certainly magnificent. The strata give the Thames back to London and indicate a possible civic solution for analogous sites elsewhere intent on exploiting the richness of their urban context.

The theatre also gives a possible language for public buildings of all sorts when they are usually left blank on the exterior or else clothed in the clichéd monumental effects referred to earlier. At a time when even the

gloomiest of pundits intent on destroying the Modern Movement can conclude their articles with remarks about the need to rediscover the architect's 'rightful . . . role . . . that of creating a civic architecture that belongs to a distinctive public realm' Lasdun's solution to the National Theatre has a special cogency though (unfortunately for the critic in question) its forms have been evolved from the dreaded modern tradition.

The theatre is also to be praised for facing squarely the problem of institutions. Traditionally it has been one of the functions of architecture to embody shared ideals of the community in symbolic form and to give pattern of human association a suitable metaphorical framework. For this function to be carried out successfully enduring ideals and a common language of shared meanings is necessary. Neither exists today, but the need for 'a distinctive public realm' remains. The theatre offers one solution to this problem. However, as was suggested in the last section, most modern monuments fall between the stools of public communication and private authenticity. Do Lasdun's landscape metaphors cut through the prejudices against concrete or do they remain partially hermetic guiding images from his private mythology? All languages have to be learned and the strata's other qualities—especially their social richness—seem to be making their impact. Perhaps these are all ways of saying that the theatre may become a seminal building. Obviously it is premature to say. But it seems to solve problems of wider relevance than its immediate building task.

If the theatre is to have the eventual role of a prototype, it may also have the doleful position of fathering a series of bastard imitations. This will not be the theatre's fault: it is, rather, a fact of history that magnificent and unique works of art are imitated and devalued to the level of clichéd formalism. One dreads already the thought of ill proportioned strata springing up like car parks knocked askew. Admittedly this is to be pessimistic: the strata may yet encourage vital and valid transformations.

No amount of meaning in a building can make up for a lack of formal synthesis. Here the issues are the perennial ones of the art of architecture. the expression of an idea in an appropriate vocabulary, the fusion of the parts into a harmonic form, the breath of life in proportions, rhythms and textures, the choice of appropriate materials, the fusion of form, function, structure and symbol. Considered in this light, the theatre presents us with a formidable artistic resolution. This is architecture of a high order. Lasdun recently stated that among his various 'signposts' had been 'Cubism and Le Corbusier's dictum that architecture is a thing of art, a phenomenon of the emotions lying outside questions of construction and beyond them'. The theatre gives body to his words.

It is the harmony of a significant form with a significant content which contributes, in part, to the enduring work of art. Perhaps when a clear historical view of the building becomes possible, it will be relegated to some convenient and limited time span as a lyrical extension of the International Style or some such thing. My impression is that the theatre will not bob away on the sea of fashion. It touches more permanent aesthetic chords and more basic human issues than that.

Page 27: the main entrance to both theatres is on the diagonal axis of the Olivier auditorium. There is a hard, reflective elegance here that is not softened until you tread the carpets of the foyers.

Humanising the institution

Denys Lasdun
Architect of the National Theatre

Denys Lasdun has given form to the institution that is the National Theatre but he has tried not to make it institutional. He hopes that the public will use the whole building as a 'fourth theatre'.

I feel that all the public areas of the building, the foyers and terraces, are in themselves a theatre with the city as a backdrop. The National Theatre is not a temple, and the policy of the company is that it should be a very open building.

All kinds of events already happen in these parts of the building, wonderful rehearsals of 'Tamburlaine' on the terraces, kite-flying, music and people just gathering and meeting. The strata of the building are like new levels of ground and they will become real places. It is very important that the National Theatre becomes a part of the city. Any idea of a cultural ghetto has gone.

Ideally the National Theatre should become another Hyde Park Corner but I have always stressed that the role of the River Thames could become an enormous asset, and that there is a tremendous need for new housing near the theatre. Way back in 1967 in the official report to the South Bank Theatre Board, I stressed the importance of the River Thames and the

Piazza San Marco, Venice.

*need for housing. By linking the theatre to Waterloo Bridge
the essential tie with the West End of London is emphasised
but what is still needed is a community of houses, flats and
shops on the King's Reach site. I want the theatre to be
surrounded by life day and night and I hope that one day it
will stand at the centre of a regenerated part of the city.*

National Theatre terraces, London (drawn by Takashi Suzuki).

Alongside certain key photographs in this issue the
architect has written statements that express his
intentions and feelings about the building.

'*The interconnected foyers are not unlike the ancient hypostyle whose communal floors evoked a warm and lively participation by the members of its community.*' D.L.

The foyers have a gaunt, abstract presence particularly when they tower to their full height.
The complexity of the levels and foyers is intriguing and sometimes initially confusing— but the visitor is rewarded by a fascinating series of great spaces.

1

Brian Beardsmore

Detailing the drama

Any examination of the detailed design of the public spaces at the National Theatre has to respect the architect's imaginative conception of them as the 'fourth theatre'. They are rich, complex spaces that invite exploration and open vistas. The lighting, furnishing, sign posting and detailed finishes all have to fit in discreetly to the whole conception. Any analysis of these details has to be seen against the architecture which has boldly reinstated the importance of form; people are the colour and decoration.

LIGHT

There is total sympathy between the lighting and the architecture resulting from the unity of purpose of architect and lighting specialists. Richard Pilbrow and Tony Corbett brought their knowledge of stage lighting techniques to the front of house to enhance the atmosphere of the 'Fourth theatre'. It was appreciated that Lasdun did not want a two-dimensional scene but a three-dimensional place and the architecture brought to mind the drawings of Edward Gordon Craig. In Craig's drawings, the human figures are seen among looming architectural forms with raking beams of light, 1. In the National Theatre foyers Craig lives again. Some may find the lighting too gloomy in places, but it is this gloom contrasted with brightness and occasionally even glare that creates the atmosphere. The uplighting of the columns emphasising their structural function and 'splintered' surface is from a specially designed fitting recessed into the concrete floor slabs. A row of adjustable lamps is set under a

louvre—there is upward-directed light and no glare from the source, 4. In a scale to suit their high positions Concord Lighting International fittings (General Electric 12v/240W PAR 56 lamps) are clamped to a bright polished T-shaped stainless steel tube wrapped round a rectangular transformer box finished in dull stainless steel, 3. These fittings light performance photographs, posters, edge light columns and provide pools of light on the floor.

SEFT (scintered electrode fluorescent tubing—a form of cold cathode) fittings are concealed to light the central spine of the curved staircases, 4, 6, emphasising their structural form and leading the eye to the level above. Down light from the diagrid strikes the outside chamfer of the upstands and washes the concrete, 4. It is rare for such a simple element to be so effectively lit. The SEFT lighting is used again on the stairways to the Olivier, this time on the outside of the stair within the enclosing walls, and downlight from the diagrid illuminates the concrete faces of the inside of the narrow stair well. One is aware of the bright surface of the concrete but not the light source. With the exceptions of the SEFT lighting everything else is tungsten and it is by overlighting and dimming down of the tungsten that the desired warm glowing light was achieved on the concrete surfaces.

SEFT is used at low level in the bars and foyers to delineate the edge of these spaces; under the window seats, 2, and the balustrades. Here the lighting effect achieved is striking but the dark timber box housing tacked on to the concrete

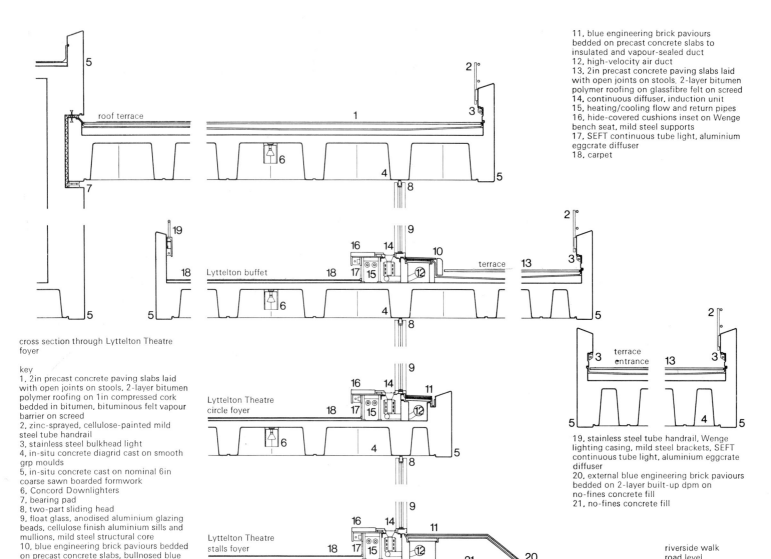

cross section through Lyttelton Theatre foyer

key

1, 2in precast concrete paving slabs laid with open joints on stools, 2-layer bitumen polymer roofing on 1in compressed cork bedded in bitumen, bituminous felt vapour barrier on screed
2, zinc-sprayed, cellulose-painted mild steel tube handrail
3, stainless steel bulkhead light
4, in-situ concrete diagrid cast on smooth grp moulds
5, in-situ concrete cast on nominal 6in coarse sawn boarded formwork
6, Concord Downlighters
7, bearing pad
8, two-part sliding head
9, float glass, anodised aluminium glazing beads, cellulose finish aluminium sills and mullions, mild steel structural core
10, blue engineering brick paviours bedded on precast concrete slabs, bullnosed blue engineering brick edging, to insulated and vapour sealed duct

11, blue engineering brick paviours bedded on precast concrete slabs to insulated and vapour-sealed duct
12, high-velocity air duct
13, 2in precast concrete paving slabs laid with open joints on stools, 2-layer bitumen polymer roofing on glassfibre felt on screed
14, continuous diffuser, induction unit
15, heating/cooling flow and return pipes
16, hide-covered cushions inset on Wenge bench seat, mild steel supports
17, SEFT continuous tube light, aluminium eggcrate diffuser
18, carpet

19, stainless steel tube handrail, Wenge lighting casing, mild steel brackets, SEFT continuous tube light, aluminium eggcrate diffuser
20, external blue engineering brick paviours bedded on 2-layer built-up dpm on no-fines concrete fill
21, no-fines concrete fill

Lyttelton buffet

Lyttelton Theatre circle foyer

Lyttelton Theatre stalls foyer

roof terrace

terrace

terrace entrance

riverside walk road level

upstand is an unconvincing detail. While it is clearly there for the lighting, was it also to provide a distance between people and concrete? The remaining parts of the lighting are stem and 'eyebrow' light bars to provide local accent lighting to display panels and lettering in the smaller spaces. The fitting used here (a new one designed and manufactured by Light Ltd) employs the General Electrical of America PAR 36 range of lamps, 5. All lighting levels are pre-set and any one of eight programmes may be selected simply by pushing a button.

SIGN POSTING
The success of the typography is the result of a close collaboration and understanding between the architect and typographer, Ken Briggs. Briggs was for many years totally responsible for the visual look of the National Theatre Company, and his posters and programmes were always outstanding. It is sad that his association with the theatre has now ended.
Legibility was paramount and Briggs was acutely aware that the typography must be a natural extension of the architecture. Lasdun and Briggs knew what they did not want, no airport look here, no Helvetica—light, medium or bold. The choice of final letter form and material came as one, 'Serifa' in brightly polished stainless steel. The silvery mirror-like quality is important, the subtle lighting casts a slight shadow on to the concrete and the letters appear to float but not leave the surface, 10. The scale is right: main titles 7in high, small titles 4in high and 3½in high battens on the staircases, 7; the elegant pictograms

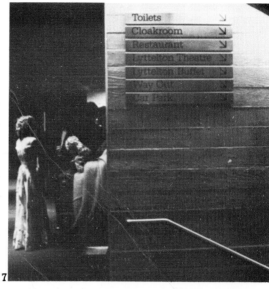

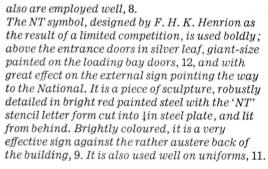

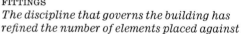

also are employed well, 8.

The NT symbol, designed by F. H. K. Henrion as the result of a limited competition, is used boldly; above the entrance doors in silver leaf, giant-size painted on the loading bay doors, 12, and with great effect on the external sign pointing the way to the National. It is a piece of sculpture, robustly detailed in bright red painted steel with the 'NT' stencil letter form cut into ¼in steel plate, and lit from behind. Brightly coloured, it is a very effective sign against the rather austere back of the building, 9. It is also used well on uniforms, 11.

FITTINGS

The discipline that governs the building has refined the number of elements placed against

the concrete to four: lighting bars, lettering, display panels and information racks, 13. Where playbills or performance photographs may be hung for maximum effect, bolt holes have been cast into the concrete to receive specially designed brackets. These brackets have been provided in just the right positions; the building cannot accept the haphazard and the theatre management must come to understand the discipline of the building. This is highlighted by the way the recent Quality of Life exhibition has been installed; crudely suspended from the ceiling, with the appearance of giant fly papers that seriously violate the building.

BARS
The bars, 14, and buffets 15, are disappointing. Service across a theatre bar has to be swift, but

other 'softer' finishes, timber and hessian. Telephone booths have veneered surfaces which have already been vandalised. Hessian wall finishes are taken right down to the carpet without protection. At the Royal College of Physicians (designed by Denys Lasdun in 1963), it was accepted that a problem existed and a flush 2½in high brushed stainless-steel skirting protects the hessian wallcovering, a detail that does its job and still looks good after 12 years. Why was the problem ignored at the NT? Was it to express the wall and floor planes with more clarity? In the box office the problem of protection to vertical timber surfaces is met and resolved by a brick plinth, 16. Yet with the information desks, which are very similar in appearance and form, the timber although recessed goes right down to the carpet, 17.

why is atmosphere allowed to evaporate here at the counters? This is partly due to the lighting, for this is the one place in the National when it does not work. Materials and colour are used arbitrarily, proportions have been dictated solely by practicalities. Oddly the cloakrooms with their low dark timber counters have more appeal than the bars.

PROBLEMS
When the architect is handling concrete, brick, stainless steel and glass, whatever the scale, he details superbly with total conviction, for the small details of his building are very important to him. For example, the simple stainless-steel clad convectors standing free from the glass and an even smaller detail, the way the architect has shaped and supported the 'original' foundation stone of the NT within his building. But there is a certain lack of conviction about the detailing of

COLOUR
In the Olivier the lavender haze of the seats is a delight with the silvery grey concrete. The colours in the Lyttelton are a variety of shades of brown; dark brown hessian walls flank the stage, the carpet is almost as dark and the seats are covered with a light beaver fabric. The curtain is a subtly contrasting dull gold. In the foyers colour is used in a totally different way, primary colours against the carefully sought-after silver grey, hazy purple field like a Poons painting. Poons does not always succeed and nor has Lasdun. The emerald green of the seats works in the Olivier spaces but not the saffron outside the Lyttelton. Yellow is difficult for painters too. The interior spaces of the National Theatre are an exciting experience, they have a pulse of their own. Lasdun has endowed his building with life. After the performance you want to linger, such is his achievement.

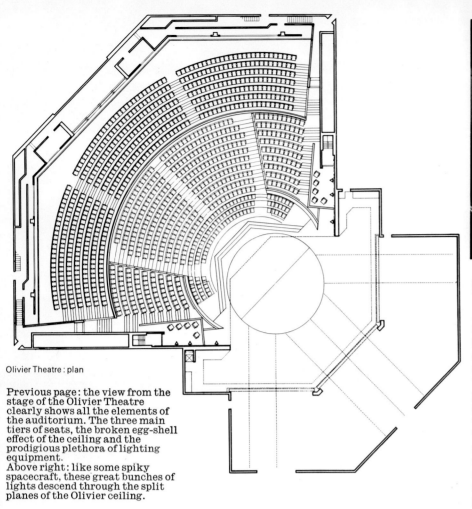

Olivier Theatre : plan

Previous page: the view from the stage of the Olivier Theatre clearly shows all the elements of the auditorium. The three main tiers of seats, the broken egg-shell effect of the ceiling and the prodigious plethora of lighting equipment.
Above right: like some spiky spacecraft, these great bunches of lights descend through the split planes of the Olivier ceiling.

Olivier Theatre

An open-stage theatre that seats 1160 people in a bowl-like configuration which embraces the stage and focuses the attention of the audience upon it. In the centre of the stage is a drum revolve, diameter 11·5 m. A large fly tower equipped with a system of power-operated spot lines covers most of the stage. There is no safety curtain. The back of the stage can be opened up or closed off to suit the scale of various productions. The front edge of the stage can be varied in shape and there is the possibility of two entrances for actors from beneath the side, intermediate tiers. Behind the stage and separated from it by soundproof doors are scene assembly spaces from which scenery can be moved on motorised wagons. The ceiling of the theatre consists of suspended elements angled to reflect sound or to mask lighting bridges.

key
1, continuous radial diffuser fabricated from 16-gauge perforated mild steel sheet stove-enamelled dark brown
2, 38 mm continuous slot
3, header box—2-seat module
4, centrally positioned 457 mm long spreader; 16-gauge perforated galvanised mild steel sheet
5, 152 mm by 102 mm inlet from plenum
6, 16-gauge galvanised mild steel sheet
7, 16-gauge mild steel sheet stove-enamelled dark brown
8, vertical supports fabricated from selected steel bars
9, holding-down bolts—machine screw fixing into expanding metal sleeve into reinforced concrete structure
10, continuous plywood scribing piece; continuous softwood edging piece fixed by main contractor to establish setting out of seat rows
11, two sheets 16-gauge galvanised mild steel, carpet covered; Carpet—contract quality 'twist' pile, colour dark brown
12, carpet—dense 'twist' pile carpet on underlay on screed; colour: dark brown
13, tip-up seat—12 mm birch-ply baseboard, 38 mm Dunlop DP 107 neomorphic foam bonded to 50 mm Dunlop DFR 168 reconstituted foam, covered wool pile fabric
14, tube and spigot pivot with nylon buffers; preformed plywood seat support
15, 101 mm wide arm rest, plywood construction on steel core, covered wool pile fabric on Dunlop DP 107 foam
16, 9 mm preformed plywood back, 50 mm Dunlop DP 107 foam covered wool pile fabric
17, plywood box construction back, 50 mm Dunlop DP 107 foam covered wool pile fabric

Seat type A:
Narrow seat without arms for the front stalls in both theatres. They are the cheap seats and they occupy the front rows of both theatres, they will provide a 'ripple' of response for the actors instead of the more usual somnolent atmosphere of the expensive front rows.
762 mm back to back; 457 mm centre to centre.
Flat floor to 203 mm riser.

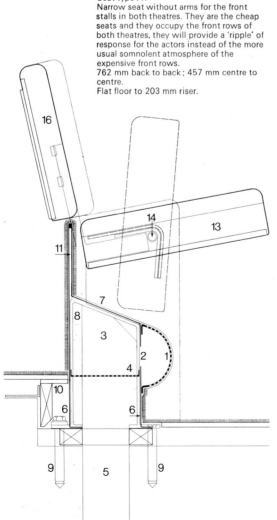

Seat type B:
Stalls seat with arms in both theatre.s 890 mm back to back; 533 mm centre to centre.
Flat floor to 317 mm riser.

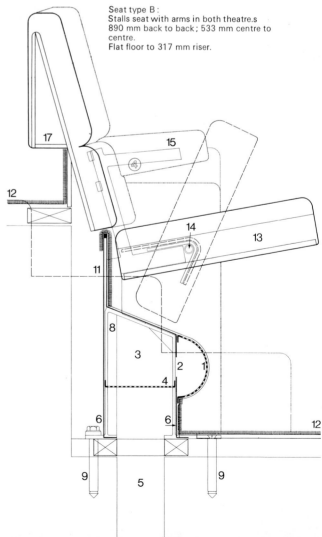

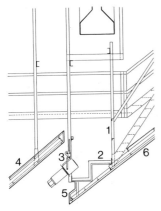
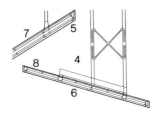
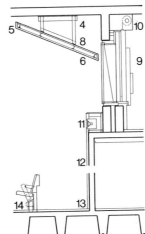

Olivier Theatre : detail section
key
1. lighting bridge
2. precast concrete floor units
3. adjustable lighting bar
4. steel-framed ceiling panels
5. fibrous plaster edge to ceiling panels
6. plaster on expanded metal
7. 2-layer plasterboard top lining
8. expanded aluminium mesh
9. projection room
10. fire shutter
11. effects loudspeaker
12. hessian-covered panels
13. carpet
14. type C seats
15. type C1 seats
16. timber rester
17. air duct from under floor plenum
18. director's room
19. electrically-operated window (1in plate glass)
20. access flooring
21. type B seats
22. type A seats
23. rising handrail

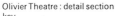
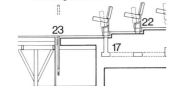
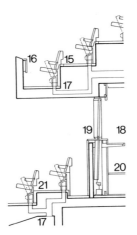

Above: auditorium seat type A.
Above right: seat type B.

Seat type C :
Balcony seat with arms in the Lyttelton Theatre and side stalls seat with arms in the Olivier Theatre.
940 mm back to back; 533 mm centre to centre.
Flat floor to 482 mm riser.

Seat type C1 :
(not illustrated)
Balcony seat with arms in the Olivier Theatre only.
940 mm back to back; 533 mm centre to centre.
Constant 571 mm.

Auditorium seats
Designed by Heritage & Race (Race Furniture Ltd) working closely with Lasdun. Variations of the same basic seat are used in both the Olivier and Lyttelton theatres. A carpeted plinth, with radial diffuser, supports a deceptively simple, very comfortable seat. It is the integration of part of the air-conditioning system with the seating that is interesting; Lasdun's starting point was a standard Race auditorium seat, its tube legs also supporting a ventilation duct/diffuser. Extensive tests were carried out by the heating and ventilating consultant, the seats at this stage were represented by pieces of plywood. Heritage modelled the seat and so a prototype stage was reached. The success of the seat we sit in, with its radial diffuser beneath, is such that we are not aware of the complexity of the problems it solves.

OVERLEAF
'We searched for a single room embodying stage and auditorium whose spatial configuration, above all else, would promote a dynamic and emotional relationship between audience and actor—between a fixed architectonic geometry of vision, acoustics and concentration and the chance irregular demands of dramatic performance. We searched for an open relationship that looked back to the Greeks and Elizabethans and, at the same time, looked forward to a contemporary view of society in which all could have a fair chance to see, hear and share the collective experience of exploring human truths. The room thus offers many possibilities and certain contradictions.' D.L.

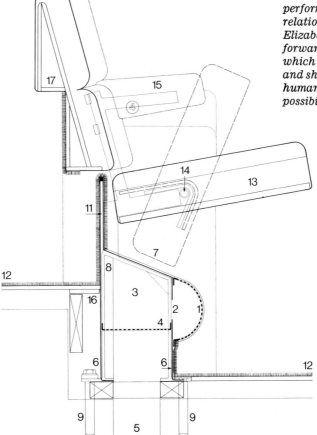

Lyttelton Theatre

This is an orthodox proscenium theatre that seats 895 people in two tiers. The proscenium arch is adjustable in width from 9 m to 13·6 m, in height from 5 m to 9 m, and on plan up to 1·6 m from the safety curtain, which is right on the forward edge of the stage. The stage can be fully raked and there is the possibility of an orchestra pit. Full-sized near and side stages, separated from the main stage by soundproof doors, are equipped with motorised scenery wagons. The fly tower over the stage has a power-operated flying system.

Comment
The decision to have long rows unbroken by gangways has led to an inevitable 'cinema feel' to this theatre. This is also because there is no messing about with boxes or 'papering the walls with people'—it is eyeball to eyeball straight-on confrontation, and very dramatic. The proscenium is strangely undefined by the architecture and much more delineated by lighting and areas of blackness. The front stalls, rows A to D, are the 'ripple' rows—the cheap seats. The carpet is dark brown and the seats a subtle 'beaver' brown.

Above and facing page (top): side-long views of the Lyttelton: from the stalls you are unaware of the circle and from the circle you don't notice the stalls, but from the 'Mappin terraces' at the sides you can see everybody.

Above: the back rows of the stalls —no disguising the concrete surroundings, the ceiling is dramatically lit from an elegant fitting.

Above: the entrance to the Cottesloe is on the east side of the theatre under the rearing concrete supports. Patrons of the Cottesloe have their own self-contained bars and foyers— all black carpets and a Corb staircase—very austere.
Facing page (bottom): looking into the black hole of Cottesloe; when in use and lined with expectant faces this could be a very exciting theatre.

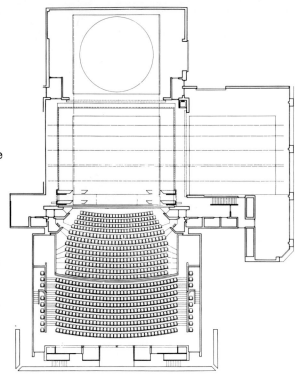

Lyttelton Theatre : plan

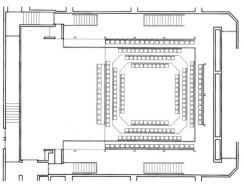

Cottesloe Theatre : in the round

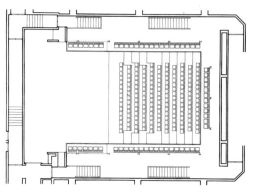

Cottesloe Theatre : end-stage

Cottesloe Theatre

This third theatre, a studio theatre for the NT company, was almost sacrificed at an early stage to save money. In 1972 it reappeared on the plans as a simple studio space which the NT company could exploit as and when money became available. In October 1973 Iain Mackintosh put forward a design study in which it was proposed to turn the space into a multi-tiered room to hold up to 400 people in a variety of arrangements. This study was then developed by the architects. The space on the plan that had to be filled was 66ft long and 56ft wide—bigger than David Garrick's Drury Lane. The solution that has been adopted has galleries on three sides, each level of the audience consisting of one row sitting and behind them a row of standing (or leaning) patrons. Depending on the stage arrangements the central floor area can take a variety of seating arrangements.
The Cottesloe can be organised inside the space defined by the three walls of galleries in a variety of ways—scenic end stage; theatre in the round; one room end stage and, by raising the auditorium in the central space to stage height and removing the lowest of the three tier fronts, a flat floor over the whole space. A moving 'fourth wall' that could vary the volume of the space and provide

a completely encircling audience has yet to be installed.

Statistics
Between 200 and 400 can be accommodated depending on layout. There are five lighting bridges and access bridges and interconnecting walkways 7·3 m above stage level. The central area between the encircling galleries is 9·9 m wide and either 9·9 m or 13·2 m long depending on whether the side gallery extensions are in use. Lighting positions are on central bridges and gallery fronts and over the end stage area. Minimal scenic suspension on hemp and winch lines is provided over the end stage.

Comment
It is too early to judge this theatre, but it does look a very promising studio theatre. In form and scale it feels like a Georgian playhouse while having an indoor Elizabethan quality that favours the non-scenic production. When it is lined by an audience it could well be an exciting cockpit for experimental productions. It is currently painted a stark black all over which gives it the air of a setting for some grim initiation or ritual. A determination to make it *feel* like a studio has deprived it of any welcoming warmth and left a great deal of the theatrical atmosphere to be provided by the plays.

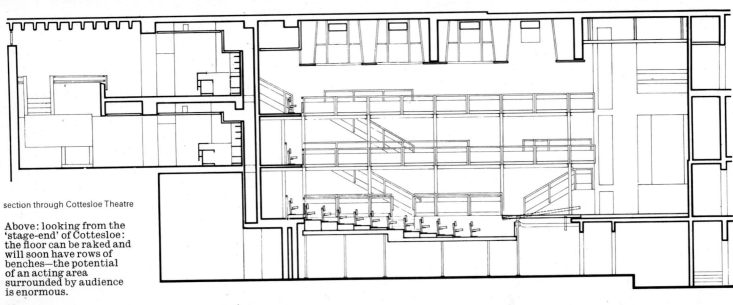

section through Cottesloe Theatre

Above: looking from the
'stage-end' of Cottesloe:
the floor can be raked and
will soon have rows of
benches—the potential
of an acting area
surrounded by audience
is enormous.

Kenneth Rowell

Scenic potential

1, Edward Gordon Craig's 'noble walls' shown in his model for *Hamlet* in Moscow 1910.

2, design by Kenneth Rowell for a mixed-media production at the new Sydney Opera House.

Any designer accustomed to working on older stages will be familiar with such difficulties as lack of stage and scenery storage space, inadequate facilities, bad sight-lines and the rest. At the National any designer cannot but be impressed with the manner in which many of these hazards have been overcome. The Lyttelton strikes one as being a contemporary interpretation of a proscenium stage, 3, providing such unusually flexible features as an adjustable proscenium and a rakeable floor. The Olivier, particularly in the bowl-like shape of its auditorium has echoes of Epidaurus, 4. Both theatres combine modern mechanics and technologically advanced equipment with Classical form. Of the two the Olivier is the more challenging to both director and designer; and it is therefore the main subject of this article. The surprising way in which this theatre manages to unite a thrust stage with a fly tower is an important development in theatres of this kind. The practical possibility here of being able to handle large scenic masses both within the area of the fore-stage and at the rear of it is the single most innovative feature of the Olivier stage. One wonders if this space, less than a theatre in the round but considerably more than an ordinary thrust stage, with its dark recesses and towering height, is the kind of ideal acting area envisaged, some 70 odd years ago, by the great Swiss innovator Adolphe Appia, who saw the stage as 'a cubic volume of space in which there takes place a continuous functioning of light'?[1]

It is tempting to predict the extent to which the very positive character of both stage and auditorium will influence future designs. It is inconceivable that designers will *not* want to exploit its spatial potential and newness. The sheer height already mentioned, for instance, makes a thrilling change from the usual brooding borders (bane of all designers) and one feels that even the vertically conceived excesses of Edward Gordon Craig's 'noble walls' would be possible here, 1.

In the past decade or so it has been directors and playwrights rather than designers who have endeavoured to redefine the nature of theatre. It was, however, designers such as Craig and Appia who, around the turn of the century, proved to be the revolutionary geniuses who not only transformed the look of our stages but inspired a totally new theatre aesthetic. In the present theatre climate it is hard to see how designers could play a

similarly important role in bringing about a renaissance in the dramatic theatre. For one thing, today's directors—though not trained designers—often exert a far greater influence on the visual style and mounting of a production. But theatres such as the Olivier ought, one feels, to be laboratories for experimenting in new scenic forms and techniques and perhaps the first question one should ask is just how much that dominant forestage will welcome scenery at all. Indeed, some of the designs already seen on this stage have looked distinctly at odds with the grey concrete walls of the auditorium and the black, functional austerity of the stage itself. It is conceivable that the architect, Denys Lasdun, has in his arena-like thrust stage created a performing area the inspiration of which was a stage that never knew scenery. Is it the eventual manouvreability of actors and scenery, furniture and props which may prove this stage's most interesting potential? Certainly the possibility of moving the action rapidly from one part of the stage to another offers both director and designer greater scope in pacing a production and making the audience feel part of the action.

Because of the absence, in the majority of our theatres, of elementary machinery with which to facilitate scene changes, stage designers have long anticipated the sophisticated mechanics of the Olivier stage—such as the drum revolve split into two semi-circular sections. It has been stated that the main purpose of the machinery is to 'allow a rapid changeover from one production to another from day to day or from one production to another'. But it has also been affirmed that such devices as the drum revolve, wagons and elevators were, manifestly, the building committee's solution to the basic need to be able to change, with a maximum of ease and efficiency, scenery, furniture and props within the area roughly termed the fore-stage. If, as is happening, there are the usual delays in making the machinery operational (and this must be as frustrating for those now using the stage as disappointing for us) it is no less intriguing to imagine the fluid productions possible when all the planned mechanism is put into commission. Until then we cannot assess the efficacy of much of the basic planning of this stage. So far, of the plays that have been seen on the Olivier stage *Tamburlaine* appears to have taken into serious account the physical presence of the

3, architect's model of the Lyttelton that shows the clear confrontation of audience and 'picture-frame' proscenium.
4, model of the Olivier stage with a setting for an imaginary play that already demonstrates the strongly architectural nature of the whole space, stage and auditorium.

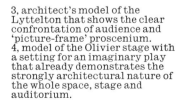

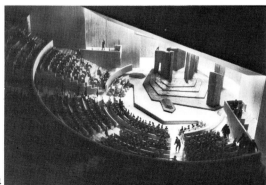

[1] see AR February 1968.

5, *Playboy of the Western World.* (Designer, Geoffrey Scott.)
6, *Tamburlaine the Great* used the shape of the whole auditorium. (Designer, John Bury.)
7, Lord Olivier on the stage as used for *Il Campiello*—actors entered from the auditorium carrying a set which was erected on this platform. (Designer, Hayden Griffin.)
8, a Russian constructivist stage design of 1921.

The complex array of lighting with which the theatre is equipped, most of it visible in the now-accepted tradition to the audience, promises much in the way of eloquent lighting design. It is conceivable that in certain future productions we may see lighting used not only to convey changing moods and atmosphere but as an increasingly powerful visual counterpart to the action. As an idea this is not new of course, but the range and power and prodigious amount of lighting equipment is exceptional here. Due to the fact that the source of much of the light is at the rear of the auditorium there is a considerable spill of light which illuminates not only the performers but also the audience. No doubt we have become conditioned to the anonymity felt in the darkened, womb-like interiors of older theatres but this light spill proves distracting and lessens the impact of the lighting on the stage itself.

A further distraction and, I think, a serious one, is the very light tone of the walls of the auditorium. The two prows or curved walls which flank the stage are ever prominent and draw the eye from the action, a further disadvantage of the light interior is that it is impossible of achieve an effective blackout. Time may show these theatres to have inhibiting factors of their own and no doubt those using the stages initially will need time to understand and come to terms with their particular characteristics. In freeing the designer of certain limitations the architects have imposed a new set of disciplines.

The reforms in scene design begun towards the end of the last century led to innovations which, in many ways, we continue to exploit today. Naturalism, Symbolism, Constructivism, Realism, Romanticism—the stylistic range and permutations are endless— all exert an influence on today's designers. Despite the international vocabulary of much scenography certain national characteristics are to be found. Many imaginative settings were created by the Neo-Romantic designers and painters in England in the 1950s. Leslie Hurry, Sophie Fedorovitch, John Piper and Loudon Sainthill were among those whose work was highly individual in style. More recently English design has tended towards the example established in other countries, in which a far greater pre-occupation with new materials and textures is to be noted, 2. Somewhat belatedly our designers and directors have permitted themselves at least a nodding acquaintance with—for example— Constructivist, 8, and Brechtian ethics.

In mounting period plays, though, English designers have often displayed a real knack in distilling the essential characteristics of a period; not surprisingly this is particularly the case in the matter of English historical drama. There is no doubt that, in time, the National Theatre stages will be used by designers of widely varying styles. An eclectic wide-ranging spectrum of design is preferable to a 'house style' and can only add to the richness and variety of the productions. Peter Brook, Grotowski and others have shown that you can take a space, any space, and create theatre. That is a thrilling and valid concept, but it does not mean that we do not also need beautifully planned and efficient stages on which to work—the new theatres at the South Bank provide them.

stage and auditorium, so indivisible in this theatre, 5. *The Playboy of the Western World,* which was designed for the Old Vic stage, sits uncomfortably in its new setting, 6. Naturalism, acceptable when distanced by the proscenium arch, has always been a dangerous game on an open stage, as it is essentially a style belonging to the theatre of illusion. A form of heightened realism depicting in some detail elements of the environment has, so often in the past, proved more convincing and expressive on this kind of stage. *Il Campiello* was, on the other hand, designed for the Olivier stage yet the design makes no attempt to explore the volume of the stage space to suggest the Venetian square required by the text. Further, the use of painted cloths caused one to think of operatic scenery of the nineteenth century, a somewhat gratuitous snub to the brand new theatre, 7.

Breaking the formal concept

Peter Hall, director of the National Theatre, talks to Colin Amery

The National Theatre opened in spasms during 1976 and when the Queen declared the building open on 25 October 1976 only the Cottesloe Theatre, the smallest auditorium, was awaiting completion. The building's opening coincided with the economic depression and the national nervous breakdown and so it received a very mixed reception. The director, Peter Hall, faced a barrage of criticism. He was urged to economise, to spend less on bureaucracy and to leave the Arts Council some money to spend in the regions. Hall answered some questions from Colin Amery across his glass-topped desk at the theatre.

CA: Do you feel a bit like a street-arab that has strayed into the Hilton when you are in this building during these hard times?

HALL: *I suppose in comparison with a lot of older buildings that theatre people are used to it's very comfortable. It's not actually affluent, it's not luxuriously appointed—the finishes are utilitarian. I can understand that many people feel that the National will run away with too big a share of the Arts Council's money for the theatre. That hasn't happened yet and it mustn't happen. The National Theatre will create new talent and new audiences and therefore new energy but just now everyone understandably has a hair-shirt attitude to all aspects of life in Britain.*

CA: You know that quotation from Granville Baker that is always cropping up, saying that a National Theatre should be a visibly popular institution; do you feel that the architecture here is helping the NT to become a popular institution?

HALL: *Yes, I think the architecture helps a great deal. As an architect, Lasdun is working in a medium that is, just now, unpopular with many people. Have architects ever been so unpopular as they are today? At the National Lasdun is also working in a style which because it is monumental outside is regarded by those who've not been inside as perhaps a little inhuman. But he's succeeded in making it work because the scale is correct: it is human. His foyers depend upon being thronged with people. People immensely enjoy being in the building: they are drawn to the magnificent city views and the exciting spaces. It may to some look too splendid, even formidable from outside. I would say it has grace and proportion. And inside it's marvellously human.*

CA: The Olivier auditorium is perhaps *The* National Theatre; do you respond to its remote sources? Are you aware of the lines back to Epidaurus, to a more cosmic kind of theatre?

HALL: *Interestingly enough the building committee did not discuss Epidaurus. What Lasdun worried about was, 'what is the crucial relationship between actor and audience for you theatre people now, and in the future?' He took a rectangular sheet of paper and in one corner of it he drew a stage. He said, 'that's what you're all talking about'. And we said, 'yes and no'. 'Yes', because it did free the figure as a three-dimensional object; and 'no' because angularity is not a part of the theatre. The stage should be embraced by curves. The Olivier Theatre, though big, is intimate. Every eye in the audience is*

Epidaurus.

Victorian era (also working in repertoire) adopted all the technical devices then available, theatre construction since has been less lavish. Theatres built for West End long runs or provincial weekly repertory have a much less demanding changeover problem, and have been provided with comparatively simple stages with little or no storage space. It appeared impossible to organise a major theatre with a changing repertoire in this way. Some permanent mechanical plant, together with adequate space was essential so that the theatre could change from production to production quickly and efficiently. Time and anti-social working hours together with inflation will continue to make staff increasingly expensive and hard to recruit. Labour-saving machinery can effect economies, cut down the time needed for changeovers and thus maximise the use of the stage and auditorium for actual performance or rehearsal with the actors.

A technical sub-committee of the building committee was formed. This included the general manager, the stage director and production manager of the National Theatre Company, the architects and the theatre consultants. A number of journeys to other theatres, particularly in Europe, were made by various members of the team. By coincidence, the National Theatre Company took two productions on tour to Moscow and Berlin, which afforded a clear insight into some of the advantages of the Germanic plan of organising the rear stage spaces to facilitate changeovers in repertoire.

The key problem of the Lyttelton Theatre design was to create a proscenium or end stage theatre that would give the director and designer as much freedom in the shape and size of the stage, while always bringing the actor as close to the audience as possible. Starting from the premise of a stage of similar proportions to the sum of main stage and forestage of the Old Vic, the design proposed to include an exceptionally flexible proscenium, a flexible and rakeable floor and a full conventional flying facility. To meet the demands of rapid changeover, the concept was included of side and rear stages with wagons that could transport whole productions on to the acting area at the touch of a button, and, at a later stage, power-assisted flying was added.

The Olivier Theatre presented a more daunting problem. The shape of the stage had not yet been finalised. Many months of distinguished conversation had preceded the fundamental concept of the bowl-like auditorium facing a corner stage. The principle that the stage could be either closed in or opened out had then been agreed. But how was this stage to be shaped, both in plan and section, and how were its support areas to be organised? Again, the fundamental dimensions of the Old Vic were used as a yardstick for the overall stage size. The requirement of full scenic capability seemed to demand a fly tower, but the unusual sightlines demanded an unusual shape.

section through fly tower and drum
(scale 1 :500)

key
1. fly tower smoke outlet
2. lighting hoists
3. scenery hoist tracks at 500 mm centres
4. motor room
5. boiler room
6. fire and sound door
7. projection room
8. rear stage
9. shuttered opening to scene dock
10. workshop level
11. disc revolve
12. personnel access opening
13. drum revolve frame
14. elevator B
15. loading platform lowers under main
elevators
16. scenery access opening
17. elevator A
18. personnel understage access
19. large rehearsal room
20. rising handrail
21. removable rostra
22. acting area
23. auditorium
24. lighting gallery
25. lighting bridges
26. fly gallery
27. intermediate gallery
28. loading gallery
29. maintenance gallery
30. grid level
31. roof level

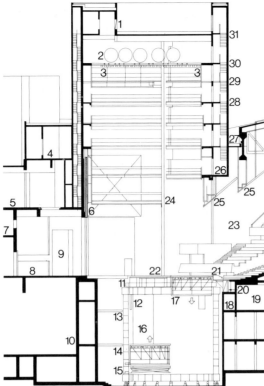

A 'stalactite' for stage and
auditorium lighting, looking
through the ceiling of the Olivier
Theatre down on to the drum
revolve (under construction).

The building committee had decided that the
fly tower should not extend to the very front of
the stage and also that, because of the great
desire to make the leading edge of the stage as
adjustable as possible, there should be no
safety curtain. The side elements of the fly
tower, occasioned by the sightlines from the
extreme side seats, had to be extended. This
led to the now characteristic shape of the
Olivier fly tower that dominates the whole
building.
Because the audience partially surrounded
the stage, a conventional flying system
restricting the suspension of scenery to lateral
lines running across the stage would be of
doubtful value. The stage seemed to demand a
'spot' or point-line flying system. We began to

search throughout the world for all available
methods of achieving this satisfactorily.
Finally we discovered that there were no
truly satisfactory systems then existing and
new developments had to be initiated to meet
the criteria that we had set ourselves. These
criteria included a system that was absolutely
safe, that could move scenery at least as
rapidly and sensitively as a human being was
able to in conventional circumstances, was
virtually silent and was capable of taking the
required estimated loads and positioning them
with great accuracy. After many months,
through the engineering expertise of Richard
Brett, the concept of employing
cyclo-convertor drives was developed. A
lengthy process of building and testing
prototypes began. The results were as
predicted. Plans were then developed for an
installation of motorised spotlines, running in
tracks across the grid, to be able to cope with
almost any contingency for flying
three-dimensional objects at any angle to the
centre line of the stage. Around the back of
the stage, it appeared logical to pursue the
side and rear stage principles already adopted
in the Lyttelton. But because of the strange
shape of the stage itself, and the constraints
of the site, these rear stage areas had to be
very compactly shaped.
The stage floor itself presented the most
perplexing problem. All were agreed upon the
need for flexibility. The shape of the stage
must be capable of easy alteration. Because
the stage in the corner of the audience room,
could upon occasion be surrounded by space,
there was need for easy access by actors from
beneath the stage at any point in its surface.
Then there was the question of the nature of
scenery that might be employed and how it
might be changed. In a conventional thrust
stage theatre—where there is no front curtain
—scenery, furniture and even properties had
either to remain static throughout the
performance, with only changes of light to
alter atmosphere or environment, or be
changed by backstage staff or actors either in
darkness or in full view. It was agreed that
while these alternatives were practical, they
were not the perfect way of operating in every
circumstance that might arise.
Our thoughts turned towards the design of a
device that would combine the advantages of
a revolving stage with wagons and elevators.
With such a device, scenery upon the thrust
stage, right in the heart of the audience, could
be lowered into the basement and turned and
replaced by new scenery or props in the same,
or any other, part of the stage. Two further
practical considerations supported this idea.
The first was that the narrowness of the
structure of the rear stage would not allow a
revolve of sufficient size to be introduced on to
the acting area by wagons as was
contemplated for the Lyttelton Theatre; and
since the Olivier Theatre was on the third
floor of the building, an alternative freight
elevator for the transport of scenery from the
workshop level below seemed essential.
Accordingly the Theta drum revolve was born
The design of the drum allows the silent
vertical or rotating movement of scenery at
an infinite number of pre-selected speeds. It
allows traps in its surface to be positioned in
an infinite number of places. Lastly, it gives
the freedom to reconstruct the thrust stage
shape very rapidly and even allows the
designer the freedom of using the space both

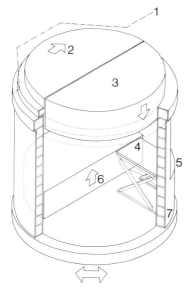

cut-away isometric of drum revolve mechanism

key
1. line of stage front
2. disc can revolve independently or lock to stage while drum mechanism revolves below
3. elevator A: can drop to basement to be replaced by elevator B(6)
4. scenery loading platform: gives access between elevator and scenery dock; lowers when elevator above drops
5. scenery door
6. elevator B: rises to stage level to replace elevator A(3)
7. drum frame: entire drum revolves on wheels at basement level

Olivier Theatre drum revolve:
sequence of movements to remove a setting and replace with new set in the same or different part of the stage
(Drawn by Tim Foster of Theatre Projects Consultants Ltd)

above and below the normal stage floor level. The Olivier Theatre, with its space and equipment, will be able to offer varied scenery in repertory economically, it will provide the director with new potential for a static or moving environment and also demand from the designer a new scenography, employing three-dimensional space to an unprecedented extent.

In the field of lighting no existing system seemed to match exactly our requirements and so 'Lightboard', a totally new control system, was conceived and engineered. 'Lightboard' is both a labour-saving device, doing away with the need for extensive patching (re-plugging) in repertoire, providing the chance for remote control focusing, and giving the designer and electrician many opportunities for speedy and efficient working in rehearsal and performance, but it is also something more. It is a lighting control system which offers to the artist far greater opportunities for the subtle manipulation of light than has been possible hitherto, that will in time extend the boundaries and possibilities of stage lighting.

Special care has been taken with the positioning of lighting positions and access to them. Wherever possible, and throughout the auditorium ceiling and walls, there is excellent access for technicians from the stage to any lighting positions. As a result of close collaboration between the architect and consultants, technical access throughout the building has been carefully considered to facilitate speedy and efficient working. Lighting equipment over the stage is suspended in a conventional manner in the Lyttelton, but on special lighting hoists in the Olivier, to allow short sections to be raised and lowered independently in order to clear the upward movement of three dimensional scenery. Suspended lighting is fed electrically by a windlass system that

automatically takes up and lets out the cable required.

The world of sound in the theatre has changed perhaps more dramatically over the last five years than any other technical department. The National Theatre sound systems employ broadcast or studio-quality engineering standards which, at the time of designing, were not used in this country at all for theatre purposes. However, the demands of the theatre require far more than simply the ability to record, albeit from a number of sound sources, and the systems offer unparalleled flexibility to allow a multiplicity of sounds to be received, processed and then broadcast at almost any point around the stages via portable loudspeakers, and the auditoria via loudspeakers built into the ceilings and walls. Last, one might move to the seemingly mundane aspects of theatrical equipment with such things as communication systems and working lights. Here, everything is aimed towards easing problems of rehearsal and ensuring speedy and efficient working and reliability in performance. The process of staging a new production can be a fraught and emotional business and is traditionally surrounded by much shouting and excitement. Hopefully, the excitement will remain but the comprehensive communication systems installed should do something to save time, irritation and screaming.

Perhaps every aspect of the National Theatre involves some area of innovation. The very scale of the enterprise itself meant that it was a first for all those involved in its creation. The flexibility of its stages and the attention to repertory planning, the sophistication of its computer-controlled flying systems and lighting with the advances in stage machinery, sound and communications combine with dozens of smaller features to make it one of the most advanced theatres in the world today.

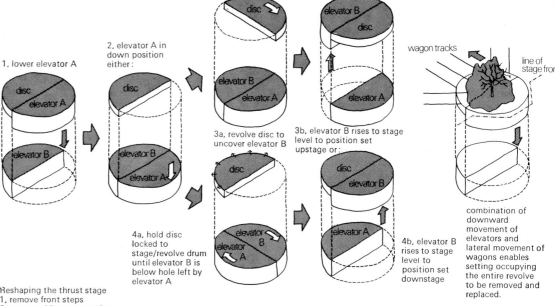

Reshaping the thrust stage
1. remove front steps
2. remove side stage sections
3. lower downstage elevator to auditorium floor level

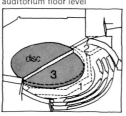

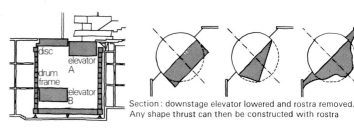

Section: downstage elevator lowered and rostra removed. Any shape thrust can then be constructed with rostra

William Curtis

Perspective

EVOLUTION OF A VOCABULARY
1, Hallfield primary school, London, 1951.
2, ground floor plan of Hallfield primary school.
3, cluster block of flats, Claredale Street, Bethnal Green, London, 1955.

The main decisions affecting the architecture of the National Theatre were made between 1964 and 1967, first of all for the National Theatre and Opera House scheme of 1965, finally for the National Theatre alone on its present site. The building therefore bears the imprint of ideas which had been guiding Denys Lasdun for nearly two decades and coincides with the maturity of his architectural language. In fact it crystallises his principles and his urban landscape philosophy. The central tenet of this outlook is that the individual building must be seen as an extension of its surroundings. Central to this idea is the extending horizontal terrace, platform or bridge bearing circulation, private or public zones. The architect hints at the meaning of these terraces when he refers to them as 'strata' in connection with the theatre. The strata have associations with landscape formations. In the theatre, at least, they are appropriate for supporting and expressing the communal nature of the building and they create 'an extension of the city'. The strata seem to be streets in the air as well as landscape levels. They are the 'fourth theatre'—a place for impromptu gatherings or events of all kinds with the cityscape as a backdrop. 'That is, the whole building is a theatre.' The strata act as public stages and auditoria simultaneously.

Moreover, the building stands in a development which has been remarkably constant in its theme and its vocabulary. It is useful to outline this vocabulary and to trace something of its evolution in the years preceding the theatre's design. Superficially, the Lasdun building is easily recognisable. It usually stresses the horizontal and is usually articulated by well-proportioned extensions of the sectional arrangement which open towards the surroundings. It tends to be sculptural and to have an overriding formal order which is cut through with a variety of spaces in sequence. Its materials and details tend to be crisply and elegantly finished. Its plan often indicates hierarchical distinction of functions and a strong sense of circulation channelling through the building from the context. There is frequently a strong correspondence between section and elevation (hence the stratified appearance) and in the work after 1960 the various levels are usually arranged in receding planes which can occur inside or outside, or both.

The main elements of Lasdun's architectural system are towers and strata. One is tempted to call this a formula but this might suggest rigid à priori procedures whereas, in fact, the Lasdun office agonises over the uniqueness of each task; if there is consistency in the results, it is because there is a consistent underlying attitude. Moreover, strata and towers are flexible over a wide range of uses. The strata are based on the technical possibilities of reinforced concrete but structure is never made a fetish in itself; it is made subservient to human use and aesthetic aims. The same is true of mechanical services and standardised components. Technology is

regarded as an instrument, not as an end in itself.

The strata serve many purposes. They support public and private zones, circulation routes and paths in and around the buildings. They can be cut through to create double and triple volumes with receding galleries and they can be compressed and opened out as compositional or functional criteria require. A recurrent Lasdun *parti* places mechanical circulation below the strata and creates a realm for pedestrians on the terrace above. The strata clearly have city-planning potential and the architect in fact refers to them as 'raised ground'.

The Lasdun system can be seen emerging through the 1950s in works like the Hallfield School, the Bethnal Green clusters, the flats in St James's and the Royal College of Physicians. This last building seems to be a watershed in which the usual concern for historical context, the problem at hand and the disparate forces in Lasdun's background achieve a synthesis. The hall with its receding strata anticipates the theatre. But between 1960 and 1965 a number of crucial experiments were made with strata on the outside of tiered buildings. Thus it is in the University of East Anglia of 1963 that the tower/strata theme is clearest, as are the landscape associations. For UEA has been conceived as a system of platforms, walkways and slopes which constitute a series of artificial hills and valleys growing off the real contours of the land.

Lasdun places considerable emphasis on direct contact with the client in the early stages when a brief is being clarified and a *rationale* evolved. A dialogue with the client has an indirect influence on the form-giving process as well as synthesising 'functions' in the mundane sense, and incorporating what the building should 'exemplify'. The kind of design process outlined here is far from the inductive methods of doctrinaire Functionalism as it is from à priori methods of reassembling elements of form over the programme. A form is found for the building task which, while it naturally draws on the experience and system of the architect, is transcended by ideas arising from the uniqueness of each site, client and job. In the case of the theatre the early discussions took place with a building committee of experts representing actors, managers, directors and so on. There was no clear, initial brief and this method soon led to the rejection of an adaptable auditorium on the grounds that it would compromise the desired high-quality relationship between audience and actors. Work proceeded on a species of open theatre and a proscenium. The method of work was the usual one for the office: discussions were all minuted and proposals were put forward by the architect in the form of balsa wood models. Such a method fits well with the design philosophy outlined above. Models are easy for the client and/or future users to understand. They are less abstracted from spatial reality than

52

drawings, and provide a suitable sculptural equivalent to Lasdun's architectural vocabulary in concrete.

Between 1964 and early 1965 schemes were evolved and tested alongside technical criteria as well as the value judgments of architect and commerce. The Olivier Theatre began life as a rectangular space with the stage and the auditorium set along the diagonal: a fixed dynamic space with a strong direction to it, but with action in the same room as the audience. The primary emphasis was on direct communication between audience and actor. Psychological, visual and acoustic qualities

continued until 1966 when the curves and side-banked seats came into the design in response to reactions against the constrictive corners of the earlier scheme. The underlying intention of a unified space with focus towards the zone of command of the stage was there from the beginning: the amphitheatre arrangement which matched this intention best was not evolved until late in the process. The proscenium theatre was brought to its final form in the same year.

In the early part of the design process (1964) the architect attempted to understand from the client and from the history of the National

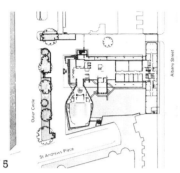

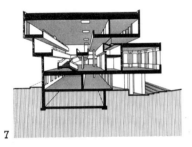

were to be paramount. This kept the capacity of the auditorium down and encouraged everyone on the Committee to shake off old habits and take risks in suggesting an ideal form.

The design process was thus an adventure from first principles. Lasdun had never before designed a theatre. He encouraged the committee to return to primary definitions. The evolution towards the final form

Theatre idea, what the building 'should exemplify'. At the same time he attempted to grasp essential, unchanging aspects of theatre and to incorporate them in his first overall scheme.

The original site for the National Theatre and Opera House was in front of the Shell Tower on the South Bank and it was a mixture of concern for counter-poising this vertical monolith, for creating a riverside metropolitan amenity and for exemplifying an ideal of a public theatre, which led to the creation of a project in 1965 composed of urban landscape terraces with extensive overhangs. The NTOP scheme arose from a full appreciation of the strata theme. It created levels of raised ground, piazzas and walks articulated by vertical fly towers. The architect's typologies were thus synthesised with the functional rationale and with his clients' and his own priorities. The scheme is known only in a balsa wood model, though,

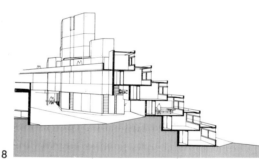

4, flats in St James's Place, London, from Green Park, 1958.
5, site plan of Royal College of Physicians.
6, Royal College of Physicians, from Regent's Park, London, 1960.
7, section of Royal College of Physicians.
8, section through a residential building at the University of East Anglia.
9, sun terrace at University of East Anglia.
10, University of East Anglia, near Norwich, Norfolk, 1962-1968.

11, one of the elevated walkways at East Anglia.
12, section through teaching buildings, University of London, 1965.

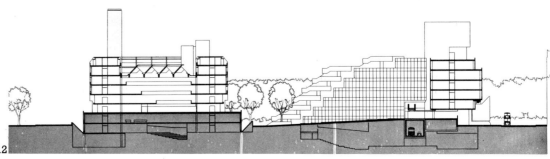

13, model of proposed National
Theatre and Opera House, 1965.
14, European Investment Bank,
Luxemburg, 1975.
15, residential building for
Christ's College, Cambridge, 1966.

16, models of early schemes for the
National Theatre.
17, model of the National Theatre,
1967.
18, detail of National Theatre
model.

undoubtedly, the finished theatre gives an
idea of what it would have been like.
The Opera House was axed in 1966. The theatre
proceeded to its present site alone. The same
priorities as before seemed pressing and
relevant so strata came once more to the fore.
Now there was Waterloo Bridge—an artery to
the West End—and so the strata were attached
to it. With the fixing of open theatre and
proscenium forms in 1966 and the design of
supporting facilities in the same period, the
final synthesis was ready. It was achieved in
1967. The most striking features of the final
plan were the expression of interior hierarchy,
the joining with public circulation, and the
45-degree inflection of the main axis. All were
typical Lasdun devices.
Technical and formal refinements continued
into the early 1970s. Models again proved their
worth in the design of details. The strata, the
diagrid ceilings, the multiplicity of joints—all
were studied carefully on models of small and
large scale. The architect's attitude to the
refinement of each building's parts is summed
up by the following:
'Every individual building will produce its
own laws and it is those laws before anything
else that an architect must understand and
accept', and 'Every building has at its heart an
image, a generating idea, which must express
itself through every part and every detail'.

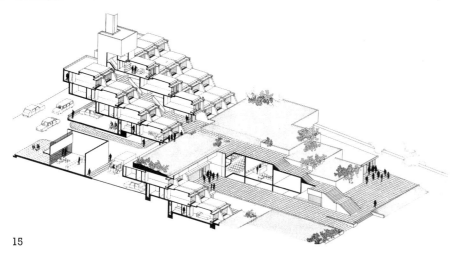

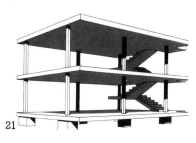

International style and other modern movement prototypes

Every work of art has its roots in tradition and each artist interprets tradition in his own way according to temperament, his own ideas and the unique problems facing him. But, as was suggested in the introduction, it is difficult to place a contemporary work in historical perspective, and this is particularly difficult at present as the whole debate on the nature of modern architecture is in a state of flux. One can nevertheless loosely indicate how Lasdun's vocabulary and preoccupations extend prototypes of earlier modern architecture, and suggest how his solution to the National Theatre relates to analogous solutions.

Lasdun was born in 1914 and his development as an architect took place before the Second World War in a period immediately following the impetus of the 'heroic' period of modern architecture in Europe. He read *Vers Une Architecture* by Le Corbusier and visited the Maison Cook and the Pavillon Suisse within a few years of their completion. He also worked with Wells Coates and Berthold Lubetkin, both architects at the spearhead of the English modern movement, both heavily indebted to European developments and both working within the framework of the International Style. A house which Lasdun designed in 1938 in Paddington was conceived as a homage to Le Corbusier. With its strip windows, flat roof, simple geometrical form, and *pilotis*, it represents a re-working of the French architect's system for concrete 'The Five Points of a New Architecture': 1 Pilotis; 2 Free plan; 3 Free facade; 4 Roof terrace; 5 Strip windows. Simplicity of form, the use of concrete and glass, the new sense of space and a concern for a suitable setting for modern life, became basic preoccupations for Lasdun. In all the later work one recognises echoes of

these themes and of the white geometrical shapes articulated by areas of dark glazing of the International Style. In particular, the architect was concerned with finding a vocabulary based on the potential of reinforced concrete. It is instructive to compare the system of the theatre—strata and towers—to Le Corbusier's 'Five Points', or their source diagram, the Dom-ino system of point supports and cantilevered slabs of 1914. Le Corbusier's system is regular, has evenly extending slabs, is amenable to mass production, has no need of supporting walls, creates free planning opportunities and suggests a grid type of plan: one sees him experimenting with this system from the villas of the 1920s to the monuments at Chandigarh in the 1950s. Lasdun's system, on the other hand, has its slabs joggled this way and that, extending back and forth. It has uneven spacing in vertical and horizontal directions and opens up at the edges where overhanging cantilevers and strata extend towards their surroundings. It has as its

vertical supports towers and directional piers and the space is free-flowing. Finally the pervasive image is one of landscape.

To Le Corbusier, the concrete frame also had urbanistic possibilities. It is instructive to consider the strata principle of raised ground alongside Le Corbusier's element, the roof garden, and his Algiers scheme of the 1930s, where the streets, gardens and houses of a city have been inserted into an extending concrete frame of *terrains artificielles*. The form is certainly different from the theatre, but the idea is analogous.

Lasdun was also influenced by Wright's 'organic' sense of space and form. In the overhangs of the theatre, the 45-degree protrusions, the stratification and the rich sense of volumes extending inside to outside, one recognises an extension of the prairie house formula, with its spreading horizontal eaves and long, low lines echoing the ground plane. The closest analogy though is from Wright of the 1930s, the Kauffman House at the Bear Run ('Falling Water'), where stratified extensions of the natural rockface blend the literal and the metaphorical. What is lacking in Wright's pastoral romanticism is Lasdun's celebration of the city and the public realm. Thus it can be seen that Lasdun has evolved his vocabulary from the prototypes of the 'modern masters'. That the results are not clichéd imitations is testimony to the functional disciplines which went into their creation, the authenticity of the ideas which underlay them and the atmosphere of questioning of modern architectural prototypes in the post-war period.

Post-war urbanism and architectural parallels

Lasdun's work of the 1950s exhibits a gradual departure from the work of predecessors as, bit by bit, the language and theme began to emerge, Hallfield School and the Bethnal Green clusters thus exhibit mannered Lubetkinisms, but their organisation indicates a quest for a flexible plan form based on circulation and sensitivity to context. The clusters, with their vertical wings of maisonettes attached to a core of vertical circulation by bridges, indicate an attempt to turn a Bethnal Green street on its end. A high-rise ideal derived from CIAM urbanism is thus modified to respond to local social conditions and what the architect called 'the grain of the surrounding area'.

While this strategy was one which Lasdun came to on his own with the help of urban theorists like Kevin Lynch, it was one towards which other architects of the period were aspiring. The position was vaguely this. There was a modern movement whose visions, techniques and imagery still provided an inspiration, but which seemed no longer to embody the ethos of the post-war period, and which seemed especially rigid and absolute with regard to the problems of the city. There ensued a period of re-working prewar prototypes—and the great post-war example of the Marseilles Unité d'Habitation—into flexible forms responding to unique sites, cultural situations and building tasks.

The strata, like the street deck, has roots in Le Corbusier's various attempts at making streets in the air and in his concern to utilise the roof terraces of his communal buildings for gardens, social spaces and areas of leisure. Like the strata, the street deck was—in

25, 'Falling Water', by Frank Lloyd Wright, 1936.
26, roof terrace of l'Unité d'Habitation, Marseilles, by Le Corbusier.
27, boardmarked concrete at l'Unité d'Habitation.
28, entrance ramp at the Carpenter Centre for the Visual Arts, Harvard University, by Le Corbusier, 1960.
29, Salk Institute, laboratory buildings La Jolla, California, by Louis Kahn.

theory at least—concerned with the social idea of 'the street as agreement' (to paraphrase Kahn) and was to exist on the *edge* of the building thus facilitating a visual and psychological link with the surroundings. But there the similarities cease: the street deck was not to be arranged in tiers, set-backs or spatial layers, it was not to penetrate to the heart of a building, and was less likely than the strata to create places to stop and linger. Metaphorically the street deck did not imply references to landscape and visually it was far less interesting than the strata in terms of both form and view.

The primacy of circulation and the emphasis on platforms in the theatre, do find parallels in two works of the early 1960s—one still a project, the other partially completed: The Venice Hospital scheme by Le Corbusier and the Berlin University development by Josic, Candilis & Woods. But in neither of the schemes is there the same interest in hierarchy that the theatre exhibits, and neither is as monumental. Moreover, the Berlin scheme fails to express adequately in its elevations the strength of its plan idea. Another vein of tradition into which the theatre seems to fit is one that may be called 'Modern Primitivism'. One sees echoes of this fundamentally romantic and rustic strain in Le Corbusier's late works with their *beton brut* finishes, their rejection of machine age slickness and their ancient look. One senses something of this sensibility too in the later works of Kahn and, in an exaggerated formalist way, in Rudolph. At its best, 'Modern Primitivism' embodies the sense of the new and the old simultaneously and suggests that the aims of architecture do not change very much, only the means. To have thought out a major monument in terms of rocky outcrops of strata, is to have taken a fundamentally primitivist stance.

Touchstones in nature and earlier traditions
Enough has been said to indicate that Lasdun, with his partners Redhouse and Softley, have rejected the mechanical analogy and replaced it with naturalistic analogies, particularly references to earth formations and landscape. Moreover, Lasdun's architecture has touchstones in traditions earlier than the modern movement. The work of Nicholas Hawksmoor has been a constant inspiration and this is perhaps visible in elaborate, highly plastic details, dramatic towers and silhouettes, soaring white forms and contrasting shadows. In the theatre particularly, there are features which recall the Baroque: a flowing sense of forms which unites all details in a larger whole, and a fusion with the surroundings. Classical reminiscences are strong, especially in the rule of proportion.

The strata have obvious parallels in ancient architecture but it is difficult to know whether the architect has been directly influenced by these precedents. Sequences of terraces, courts, ramps and levels traversed by processional routes recur in early Mesopotamia, Egyptian, Mezzo-American and Far Eastern architecture, usually in sacred and monumental complexes. It is probably correct to see this as a mere parallelism: the strata are innocent of any self-conscious attempt at digging up ancient prototypes. Working through modern means, they suggest fundamentals.

The National Theatre idea and the problem of monumentality
The National Theatre solution responds to the aspirations of both client and architect: the inclusion of two main auditoria of fixed and specific character with a flexible studio was a joint decision and while the forms of these theatres were generated by the architect, they were constantly checked alongside the building committee's criteria and reactions. The form of the building as a whole, on the other hand, issued from the architect's world: we have seen how clearly it represents premises he had been clarifying for over two decades. But the inflexions and meaning given to strata and towers at the theatre arise too from the architect's consultation of what he sensed his client thought a national theatre should exemplify. At a deeper level, it is possible he was able to tap some of the essential realities of theatre and to reinterpret the idea of a theatre. The building certainly attempts to give the institution a suitable monumental and symbolic framework.

Lasdun's response to his brief reveals something fundamental about the nature of the institution of theatre and its human meaning. Lasdun's solution stresses that a theatre is first and foremost a public building: a fragment of the public realm for performance, gatherings and celebrations, a place where dramatic experience is shared. The strata celebrate this basic definition and respond to its communal and ritualistic implications.

The theatre is part of the city, the city part of the theatre. Street and square were the earliest urban settings of drama and there is a return to street theatre when events occur (either planned or spontaneously) on the 'fourth theatre' of the strata. As levels of landscape, they recall equally the earliest rural setting of theatre—the side of a slope or a bank. The theatre addresses the unpopular questions of rhetoric and monumentality as well as the public definition of theatre. The creation of monuments is difficult for the modern architect for many reasons. First of all, they seem to be regarded as an embarrassment. Secondly, the modern movement has removed some of the standard means for monumentalising: the iconography of domes, porticoes, grand orders, of stressed entrances, axial symmetry and honorific materials, public figurative sculpture and painting. Such devices could be put to use to evoke parallelisms with grand, well-known monuments of the past and to express civilised ideals which commanded immediate response from the public even at the crudest level of understanding.

But by its various rejections, the modern movement put paid to such direct re-use of past images and forms. The very language of modern architecture has tended to blur distinction of civic hierarchy behind uniform facades of glazing or strip windows. Moreover, the spatial expression of modern economics and services tends to create a cityscape emphasising abstract functions and circulation at the expense of place and symbolism.

Some of the traditional semantics of monumentality have come in through the backdoor in many disguises and the results are rarely encouraging. The dilemma is illustrated by complexes like the Lincoln

30

31

32

ROOTS
30, tower of St George's in the East by Nicholas Hawksmoor, 1723.
31, Mayan pyramid of Kukulcan, Chichen-Itza, Yucatan, Mexico, New Empire period.

Center in New York where axial planning, formal symmetry, the geometrical control of open spaces, veiled references to the Classical tradition and expensive materials are used to suggest the hierarchial importances of the building within the cityscape. The message is bound to be confused in an environment of towering skyscrapers which make the building look like a desk-top ornament, but

the real problem is that the results smack of high camp. The result undoubtedly communicates the message, I am a monument, but from the architectural point of view it is a cheap effect.
Part of the problem is that there is no fixed symbolism for buildings of *any* function any more. If the architect returns to previous styles and imagery for the institution for

33

34

MONUMENTALITY
32, Sebastiano Serlio, woodcut of a *scena tragica*, 1545.
33, main stairway of the Opéra, Paris, by Charles Garnier, 1875.
34, Andrea Palladio's Teatro Olympico.
35, Le Corbusier's project design for the Palace of the Soviets, 1931.
36, Parliament buildings at Chandigarh, by Le Corbusier, 1955.
37, chapel at Ronchamp, France, by Le Corbusier.

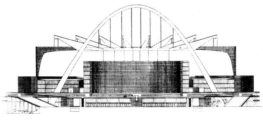

35

which he is trying to find a form he usually lapses into banality. If he does not, he runs the risk of not communicating—unless his control of architectural space is such as to evoke the seriousness of the institution. Here one thinks of the undoubtedly private language of Le Corbusier's Ronchamp which by means of its shape, pre-existing associations with its site, processional routes, stained glass, some standard elements of church furniture and the creation of a mystical space, still succeeds in conveying its meanings without lapsing into inauthenticity. Unfortunately, such a bridging of the gap between private invention and public understanding is rare.
In such schemes as the League of Nations, the Palace of the Soviets projects, and the Mondaneum, Le Corbusier attempted to evolve monumentality with an authentic modern vocabulary through the creation of hierarchies, giant sequences of space, landscaping and the grandiosity of structure. These experiments were continued in the post-war period and culminated in the monuments at Chandigarh. In the Parliament building, for example, the hierarchy of the interior chambers is indicated by vast forms in light. Grandeur is reinforced by the placement of the building as a free-standing object on a

36

37

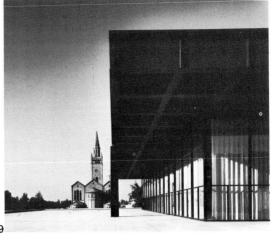

38, Boston City Hall, by Kalman McKinnel, Knowles, 1964.
39, National Gallery, Berlin, by Mies van der Rohe, 1968.

plateau silhouetted against a majestic, distant landscape. Within the building, primary geometrics, repeated elements, the vastness in scale of the peristyle spaces of the interior halls, the ascending ramps and the control of light on a sculptural form, communicate a highly serious intention. Bare concrete, with its evocation of worn stone and ancient ruins, is capable of giving a sense of the permanent, the non-slick and the perennial. That there are historical references at Chandigarh is beyond doubt— the massiveness, the giant forms and the processional ways must all have been culled from the 'Lesson of Rome' or the architect's understanding of the monumental

organisation of the past, but the building remains a modern work.
To return to the National Theatre: how can it be evaluated in the context of monument-making? The large scale of the towers, the uninterrupted treatment of the strata, the geometrical control of the entire form, the use of axes and processional routes, the elegance and forthrightness of materials, the expression of hierarchy and partial symmetry (especially the manner in which the monolithic circulation towers flank the main entrance)—these are all ways in which the theatre proclaims its importance in the city hierarchy. There is grandeur of effect with simplicity of means.

Iain Mackintosh

'Scene individable or poem unlimited'

'Going round by way of Lambeth one afternoon in the early summer of 1870, we had skirted the Thames along the Surrey bank, had crossed the river higher up, and on our way back were returning at our leisure through Westminster; when, just as we were approaching the shadow of the old Abbey at Poet's Corner, under the roof-beams on which he was so soon to be laid in his grave, with a rain of tears and flowers, he abruptly asked—"What do you think would be the realisation of one of my most cherished day-dreams?" Adding, instantly without waiting for any answer, "To settle down for the remainder of my life within easy distance of a great theatre, in the direction of which I should hold supreme authority. It should be a house, of course, having a skilled and noble company, and one in every way magnificently appointed. The pieces acted should be dealt with according to my pleasure, and touched up here and there in obedience to my own judgment; the players as well as the plays being absolutely under my command. There," said he, laughingly, and in a glow at the mere fancy, "*that's* my day dream".'

The day dreamer on the South Bank was Charles Dickens. In 1848 Dickens had thanked Effingham Wilson for his pamphlet on a National Theatre, wishing his project well but adding 'I wish I could cherish a stronger faith than I have in the probability of its establishment on a national footing within fifty years'. Dickens' scepticism was understandable: the very concept of a national theatre was foreign to the English theatre of the nineteenth century. If anything it suggested state controlled monopoly which had been abolished under the 1843 Licensing Act that allowed any licensed theatre to present legitimate drama which hitherto had been reserved exclusively to the patent theatres of Drury Lane and Covent Garden. Indeed, even after 1843, lessees of Drury Lane during the nineteenth century often claimed the title national theatre when presenting a new policy or new building to London playgoers. Augustus 'Druriolanus' Harris issued a leaflet in 1885 reminding his public 'that Drury Lane has been known from time immemorial as the National Theatre', and setting out his achievement over his first six seasons which, in addition to productions of Shakespeare and Wagner, included a visit in 1881 of Europe's finest Classical ensemble, the Saxe-Meiningen players.
Earlier Samuel Beezley, architect, had commemorated his total rebuild in 1822 of the stage and auditorium with a plaque announcing: 'The interior of this national theatre was entirely pulled down and rebuilt in the space of fifty-eight days' (modern contractors please note). Yet the soubriquet of National for Drury Lane was spurious: it might have been merited during Garrick's tenancy from 1747 to 1786, but had long since been abused by those who favoured spectacle in place of drama, scene rather than poem.

Indeed the author/critic Richard Cumberland had summed it up in a sentence when both the patent houses, Drury Lane and Covent Garden, had by 1806 been rebuilt at two or three times the scale, without their full fore stages and without proscenium arch doors: 'Hence forward theatres for spectators rather than playhouses for hearers . . . the splendour

1

of the scenes and the ingenuity of the machinists and the rich display of dresses aided by the captivating clamours of the music now in a great degree supersede the labours of the poet'.
Back to Dickens in 1870. We now know that it would be a century before Britain had a house 'in every way magnificently appointed'. But for over 60 years Britain has had not one 'skilled and noble company' but two. One was housed at the Old Vic where Lilian Baylis first

2

1, Saturday night at the Victoria Theatre, an illustration from *The Graphic*, 26 October 1872.
Old Vic 1872-1927
2, this view of the Old Vic taken on the occasion of a visit to the theatre by the Prince and Princess of Wales on 3 March 1910 shows (as does 1) the sort of actor/audience relationship that many modern architects would envy. Only the Cottesloe in the new National Theatre, Christ's Hospital School Theatre (AR February 1975) and Eden Court Theatre, Inverness (AR October 1976) have anything approaching this sort of intimacy.

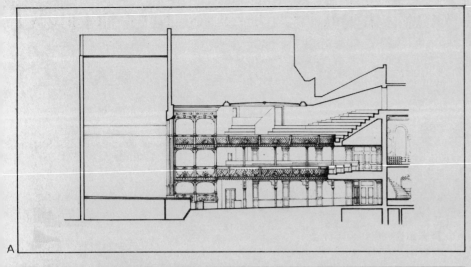

A

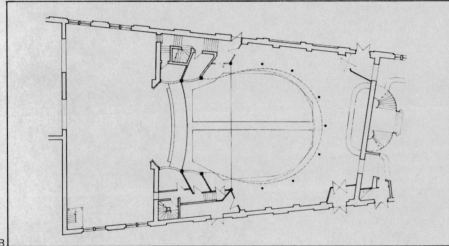

B

The Old Vic 1871-80: A, section; B, plan (scale 1:500 approx)

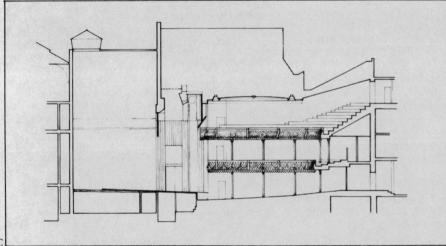

C

The Old Vic 1976: C, section; D, plan

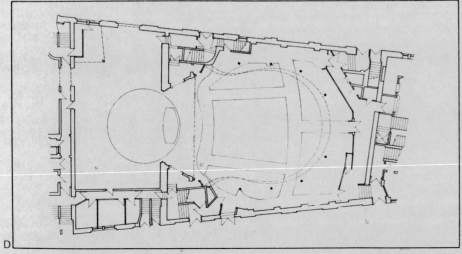

D

presented Shakespeare in October 1914 and the other at Stratford where Frank Benson first presented a season in 1886 in the original theatre, opened in 1879 and burnt down in 1926. Both companies evolved were of international stature and, in that they both honoured England's national playwright William Shakespeare, could both lay claim to being national companies. In both theatres money was always scarce and the need for any improvements had to be carefully weighed both by Governors and by whoever was in command of the company. At one the building burnt down and a new theatre had to be commissioned, a process that might suggest positive thinking as to how to design a national theatre. Indisputably both companies were substitute national theatre companies and the purpose of this article is to examine how these relatively simple playhouses, Old Vic and Stratford, fared as substitute national theatres until the arrival of the real thing in 1976.

The Old Vic is the smaller and the older of the two. It was opened as the Royal Coburg Theatre on 11 May 1818 (reassuringly to us today 'in a still unfinished state'). While there is nothing recognisable left of the original interior by Rudolph Cabanel, two relevant points can be made about that arrangement: first that within the same four walls as exist today Davidge, manager from 1824 to 1833, could accommodate over 4000 (capacity in 1976: 948); second that in presenting Edmund Kean at the Royal Coburg in 1831 Davidge could contrast his *small* playhouse with the vast 'theatres for spectators' of Drury Lane and Covent Garden:

'Those of the Theatrical public who have hitherto only witnessed the efforts of this great Tragedian in vast spaces of the Patent Theatres, will find their admiration and delight at his splendid powers tenfold increased by embracing the present opportunity of seeing them exerted in a Theatre of moderate dimensions allowing every Master look and fine tone of the artist to be distinctly seen and heard'.

The theatre was still of moderate dimensions when it was acquired in 1880 by Emma Cons who, by succession through Lilian Baylis, her niece, has bequeathed to us the Old Vic and its curiously complex living tradition. The Old Vic in 1880 bore little resemblance to the theatre of Cabanel but a great resemblance to what survives today. Most history books have got it wrong: the present interior was originally laid out by J. T. Robinson, architect, and dates from 1871. The plans that have been the basis of the earlier pair of redrawn plan and section are in the GLC archives: the plan being signed by J. T. Robinson and dated 19 July 1871, the section being dated 1880 and drawn by E. Hoole, architect. After the 1871 reconstruction new owners had renamed the theatre the New Victoria Palace. A few years later they had to sell and at the sale the capacity of the 'noble, lofty and well ventilated auditorium' was said to be 2300 with a possibility of seats for 500 more. At the lower level there were 560 pit seats with a promenade for 400, and it is this layout, attractive to modern eyes, which is illustrated.

The first pair of drawings, A, B, establish the stage and auditorium that Emma Cons acquired in 1880. The second pair, C, D, show the theatre as it exists today virtually

Old Vic 1928-1941
3, the proscenium arch as altered by Frank Matcham who had never built horizontal tier fronts into any of his 100 plus theatres. Hence the writhing box fronts that straightjacket the proscenium. No more unbroken shelves of humanity running right to the stage to the point where the actor can touch the play-goer in the stage box. This was the Vic that Tyrone Guthrie ran from 1933-1936.

3

Old Vic 1951-1960
4, Architect Douglas Rowntree and stage design consultant Pierre Sonrel gave the Vic a clean, fiftyish look. There was now a pronounced throat effect—which produced a no man's land. The director was Michel St Denis.

4

Old Vic 1960-1962
5, Michael Benthall as director minimised Sonrel's throat effect by reintroducing the style and finishes of the auditorium into the no man's land. Uneasy junctions hide behind two giant Corinthian columns—definitely the *Romeo and Juliet* version.

5

Old Vic 1962-1963
6, no full frontal view survives but this photograph records the short-lived tunnel proscenium devised by Michael Elliot and designer Richard Negri. This novelty had no time to wear off, the Old Vic Company gave its last performance in June 1963.

6

Old Vic 1963-??
7, the National Theatre Company move in and Sean Kenny tries to replace one proscenium with another 14ft (4·25 m) further downstage and 14ft (4·25 m) wider than the old one (28ft 6in wide (8·68 m)). This solution fails to take advantage of the uniquely intimate actor/audience relationship that could be achieved in this theatre and should be regarded as temporary. As the Old Vic is the one theatre in London with both the architectural form and the theatrical tradition that makes it ideal for a simple staging of the classics—why not a return to the arrangement of 1871?

7

untouched since the last major alterations made for the reopening by the National Theatre Company on 22 October 1963. What happened in between is shown in 3-7. The photographs tell an interesting story: while the form of the auditorium, two horseshoe tiers over a large pit, has remained relatively unscathed, the character of the transition from auditorium has changed again and again as the tide of theatrical fashions has ebbed and flowed. Many of the improvements were part of a package commissioned for some other purpose: in 1928 to meet certain LCC requirements following the rehousing of Morley College which used to occupy most of the fly tower and stage basement; 1951 to repair war damage; 1963 to accommodate the National Theatre Company. But on none of these occasions was it necessary to alter the proscenium arch zone: it was done because the men in command wanted it altered. As a footnote it ought to be added that somebody did once consider gutting the auditorium, the somebody being none other than Lilian Baylis in 1927. Only Ellen Terry could have uttered this reproof to 'the lady': 'if you allow the circles to be altered, I will haunt you, alive or dead'. Sadler's Wells, built by Baylis in 1931 as much for drama as for opera and ballet, suggests the catastrophe that was averted at the Vic.

The Stratford Memorial Theatre is much younger than the Old Vic but has been much more extensively altered. While at the Vic 1871 is still the dominant mood of all but the proscenium arch zone, at Stratford almost every feature of Elizabeth Scott's 1932 auditorium has vanished. The comparative set of drawings overleaf show that the walls of narrow fan of the auditorium remain in plan as they were originally set out and that the proscenium arch remains unaltered in width, this being 29ft (8·8 m), almost the same as at the Old Vic. But there the similarities stop for not only have all the surface finishes been changed but also the very arrangement of the audience itself. The change is total and yet at no time has the theatre been totally reconstructed. Dozens of minor changes have cumulatively transformed a bare, sparsely populated, clean finished 1930's scenic theatre into a busy, bursting, focused, galleried playhouse in which it is possible to fuse audience world and actors' world into a single theatre space. In the course of this evolution the seating capacity has increased from 1000 in 1932 to 1576 in 1976. It is interesting to note that each improvement advocated on the grounds of actor audience relationship has had a box office pay off: of no other twentieth-century theatre can it be said that architectural and theatrical improvements have resulted in an increase in capacity of over 50 per cent.

Elizabeth Scott's original design would never have been built had the client, the governors of the Memorial Theatre, been in command. But they had opted for an RIBA-organised competition held shortly after the fire of 1926. They had to live with the jury's decision announced in the autumn of 1927. The unfortunate architect had had a skimpy brief beyond the governors' pious exhortation to design a building 'simple, beautiful, convenient, a monument worthy of its purpose'.

After Elizabeth Scott had won, a technical committee was appointed, led by designer

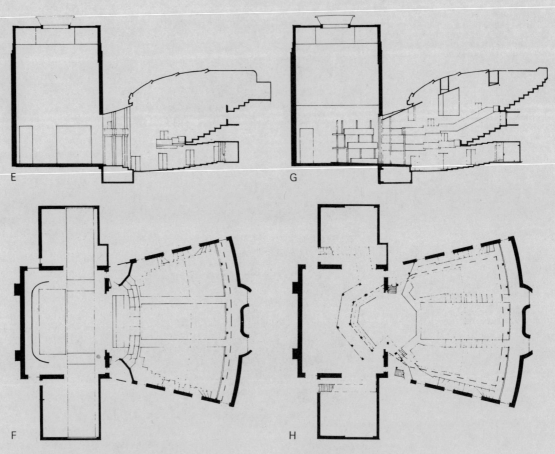

Stratford-upon-Avon 1932 : E, section;
F, plan (scale 1 :600)
Stratford-upon-Avon 1976 : G, section;
H, plan

E

G

F

H

Norman Wilkinson and manager Barry
Jackson. They did what they could to make
the building workable backstage. Meanwhile,
in the auditorium the governors got the sort
of bleak '30s theatre that was familiar in
Europe but was exceptional in England.
There was criticism. Beachcomber called it
'the new Soviet barracks at Stratford'. During
the Second World War, Herbert Farjeon
declared 'that if the next bomb dropped by a
Nazi raider on a public building in this
country were to fall on the Shakespeare
Memorial Theatre, the bones of the Bard
might not lie uneasy in that unopened grave'.
Theatre people on the whole hated it and said
so after the opening celebrations were over.
The AR, on the other hand, loved it.
Some quotes from the AR of 1932, in which it
was suggested that three things determined
the character of the 1932 theatre. First, perfect
sight lines: 'We are in a theatre in which the
auditorium is in a broad arc. No pillars
interrupt, there are no boxes; from every seat
the stage can be seen . . . it provides everything
the spectators need for seeing (including very
comfortable seats).' Second, the acoustic
calculations: 'The shape of the theatre
resembles a giant horn, and is so designed that
the players can be heard in all parts of the
stage, and the sound distributed evenly
through the auditorium. The splays, and
ceiling of proscenium, together with the
forestage when in use, act as reinforcement to
the source of sound.' Third, the modernist use
of natural materials in decoration: 'Though
new theatres continue to appear in constant
succession throughout the country each
newcomer, with a very occasional exception,
represents no more than another step along
the tiresome path of motif-ornament and
meaningless decoration. Since Palladio built
his theatre of Vicenza there has been no
development, other than an increasing
tendency towards vulgarity and over
elaboration. . . . In the new theatre at

Stratford-on-Avon materials are used with
intelligence, selection is governed by fitness of
purpose and design by the nature of the
material . . . the interior has a charm that
could never result from the application of
ornament.'
Thus spoke the AR; now for the theatre point
of view.
Actor Balliol Holloway, who led the company
for the 1934 season: 'The acreage of blank walls
between the proscenium and the ends of the
circles, coupled with the immense distance
between the lower edge of the stage proper and
the front row of the stalls completely destroys
all contact between actors and audience. It is
doubly hard on the actor that the audience
does not realise this, and is aware only of the
actor's comparative ineffectiveness.' Director
Norman Marshall, himself a leader of the new
theatre movement in the '30s, writing in 1939:
'the fundamental weakness in the design of
the Memorial Theatre is the gulf between
stage and auditorium. This would be a serious
enough defect in any theatre, but is doubly so
in a theatre built for the plays of Shakespeare
which were written for a platform stage with
no proscenium and no barrier of any sort
between actor and audience. . . . It is true that
at Stratford there is a forestage in front of the
proscenium, but it is so badly related to the
stage proper that it has every appearance of
being an afterthought. It is impossible to
combine satisfactorily a forestage and a
conventional picture-frame stage.'
All these problems were solved in the quarter
century 1951 to 1976. Anthony Quayle had been
appointed director in 1948 and, for the first
time since the days of Benson, Stratford had in
command a man of the theatre who was both
of real stature and prepared to make changes.
In 1951 Brian O'Rorke, recently appointed
architect of the projected National Theatre,
made extensive alterations. A row was added
to the leading edge of the circle, stepped boxes
were brought round at circle level to the

Stratford 1932
8, Elizabeth Scott's theatre as photographed for the AR in 1932.

Stratford 1962
9, the proscenium arch designed by Henry Bardon in 1961 and altered in 1962. The setting by Lila de Nobili is for *A Midsummer Night's Dream* directed by Peter Hall.

Stratford 1970
10, the important production of *A Midsummer Night's Dream* by Peter Brook changed the nature of Stratford—it was designed by Sally Jacobs.

Stratford 1976
11, acting area designed by John Napier and Chris Dyer arranged for *Much Ado About Nothing* directed by John Barton and designed by John Napier.

Stratford 1976
12, the stage of the Royal Shakespeare Theatre arranged for *Romeo and Juliet* designed by Chris Dyer and directed by Trevor Nunn.

forestage assemblies which were themselves totally removed. Here and everywhere the acres of wood veneer from every antipodean island were exchanged for dark paint, crimson leather, pleated material and gold studding. Capacity was now 1301 plus 76 standing. This version with minor changes lasted until 1959 and was generally liked. There was a problem: from having an over narrow proscenium at under 30ft there was now too wide an area for either actor or scenic artist to fill, some 46ft between the callipers of the new boxes. Sets spilt out sideways: what was now needed was a sense of focus. This was provided by designer Henry Bardon working closely with director Peter Hall, appointed in 1959. The result, both proscenium arch with its renaissance flavour and projecting hexagonal forestage, raked at 1 in 18, was brilliant. This arrangement was possibly the most influential conversion ever undertaken in a British theatre; the shape has recurred elsewhere and it is interesting to note that the 1976 version of Stratford creates a similar focus to a hexagonal platform thrust into a yard. The Hall/Bardon stage was modified, reclothed and reworked throughout the '60s but these were cosmetic jobs. Naturally, the theatre was never entirely happy, what theatre person ever is with a building bequeathed to him by others? Some ambitious ideas were mooted, the most fanciful being the Sean Kenny project of February 1961. Sean Kenny described it thus:

'At the moment Peter Hall and I are working on a project to redesign the Memorial Theatre at Stratford-on-Avon. of which he is director. We would like to replace the old stage and auditorium with an open amphitheatre stage, with the audience on three sides and a flying grid over the forestage. We feel this type of stage is essential if Shakespeare is to be produced properly. It would make the plays live again—they've been boxed up for too long. It would be good if the large auditorium of the proposed National Theatre in London could be built on very similar lines, so that plays could move between Stratford and London without any need for reproduction or redesigning.'
Of course, such a theatre could not fit on the narrow Stratford site. Kenny's design was reminiscent of the Saarinen/Mielziner Vivian Beaumont Theatre, New York, of 1965 and would probably have worked no better and no worse than that uneasy compromise between Guthrie-thrust and picture-frame staging. But whatever its faults, this project was a superficial influence, albeit a negative one, on the design of the Olivier Theatre some five years later.
After Peter Hall came Trevor Nunn, who took command in 1968. Until 1972 the changes were rung between 'grey boxes', 'off-white boxes' and 'black boxes' which describe masking systems within that 29ft (8·84 m) wide proscenium arch. In 1972 the penultimate change was made for *The Romans*: the balcony was allowed to extend along the still mostly blank side walls following the line below of Brian O'Rorke's circle boxes of 1951. Now Stratford bore a closer resemblance to the projected London home for the RSC, the Barbican, with its three enwrapping tiers conceived by John Bury and designed by Chamberlin Powell & Bon. Once again, as in the '50s, the scenic and acting areas was a full 46ft (14 m) wide constricted by a 29ft (8·84 m) proscenium arch 12ft (3·66 m) upstage of the

Stratford 1961
13, Peter Hall asked Sean Kenny to redesign the Shakespeare Memorial Theatre, which he did very thoroughly in this project.

stage front. It was fundamentally a scenic arrangement with the same problems of excessive width against narrow structural proscenium as has existed at the Vic since 1963. In 1976 the transformation of the 1932 design

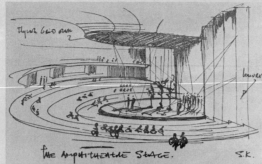

A sketch of Sean Kenny's amphitheatre stage project for the Stratford Memorial Theatre. It has a flyost grid over the stage from which scenery can be suspended.

13

was completed. The two tiers that embraced the auditorium now appear to pass through the proscenium arch which would seem to have vanished altogether, 11. Shakespeare now has a platform jutting out into the yard of what was once a cinema-like auditorium with parallel equal vision rows gazing at a small picture frame. And lest the whole story could seem a theatrical conceit one must repeat that a solution which pleases actors, directors and critics accommodates 576 more paying public for each performance than the 1000 originally accommodated in 1932. Not all are good seats, but then the prices range from £5 to £1·20, a differential of undoubted social value. Of this range of galleries John Barber wrote in the *Telegraph*: The best are peaks in Darien, and the worst offer only squatter's rights'.
Will this arrangement last? Ought it to last? Is the staging at Stratford this year merely yet another semi-permanent setting for the current season or is it a new/old acting space? Peter Brook wrote in 1968 about Stratford: 'About five years, we agree, is the most a particular staging can live'. Is it staging, is it theatre architecture that has been discussed in this article? Is it to be deplored that theatre people will always tinker with their theatres however carefully they are presented to them by the architect? Or is the tension between architects and theatre people one of the strengths of the British drama?
Perhaps to suggest that there is a tension between architects and theatre people is to miss the point. The division is more likely to be between the advocates of theatres for spectators and those of playhouses for hearers. On that divide architects and theatre people will be found on both sides. Approached from these standpoints of the supporters of 'scene individable' and of those of 'poem unlimited' one can sum up thus: At Stratford theatre people have added seats with bad sight lines to a copy book layout by Scott where everybody had an equally good view of the stage, the purpose being to improve actor audience relationship; at the Vic the demands of scenery, ot comfort and of sight lines have both reduced capacity and produced an acting area too wide for Robinson's original intimate and scarcely scenic playhouse.
The prejudice of the writer of this article is clear: pro-Robinson anti-Scott or, in other words, a vote for theatre which can 'on your imaginary forces work'. There is considerable evidence today from the underground theatre to Stratford itself of a return to bare boards and a passion. But to suggest that such a taste

for text rather than timber is also the proper one for a theatre learning to live with poverty would be dangerous because of another fundamental fact of theatre life of the last 300 years which concerns income rather than expenditure. The popular preference has been and maybe always will be for spectacle rather than poetry. Did not Garrick himself, when running England's first 'national theatre', have to change his own approach when his audience started to prefer Rich's showmanship at Covent Garden to his own Classical repertoire at Drury Lane?

'Sacred to Shakespeare was this spot design'd,
To pierce the heart and humanise the mind.
But if any empty house, the actor's curse,
Shews us our Lears and Hamlets lose their force;
Unwilling we must change the nobler scene
And in our turn present you Harlequin;
Quit Poets and set Carpenters to work,
Shew gaudy scenes, or mount the vaulting Turk,
For though we actors, one and all, agree
Boldly to struggle for our—vanity—
If want comes on, Importance must retreat;
Our first great ruling passion is—to eat'.

The evidence of Stratford reveals a gradual but inexorable shift of emphasis from scene individable to poem unlimited thereby transforming a theatre for spectators into a playhouse for hearers. The evidence of both substitute 'national' theatres indicates that an architect's auditorium, however magnificently appointed according to the taste of the day, is likely to be quickly and frequently altered as the tide of theatrical fashion ebbs and flows between 'unworthy scaffold' or 'plain built house' and 'gaudy scene' or 'noble pageant'. Lastly, theatres that aim to provide a national repertoire would appear to be more susceptible to change for good or ill than other theatres which lack an artistic director 'in supreme authority'. Did Dickens realise that it would not only be the plays that would be 'touched up here and there' according to the director's pleasure?

BIBLIOGRAPHY
Charles Dickens as Reader. By Charles Kent. 1872.
The National Theatre. By Augustus Harris. 1885.
Memoirs. By Richard Cumberland. 1896.
The Old Vic. By John Booth. 1917.
The Old 'Old Vic'. By Edwin Booth. 1917.
The Architectural Review. June 1932.
The Theatres of London. By Raymond Mander and Joe Mitcheson. Rupert Hart Davis. 1963.
The Old Vic. By Cicely Hamilton & Lilian Baylis. Jonathan Cape. 1926.
The Other Theatre. By Norman Marshall. John Lehmann. 1947.
TABS. Edited by Frederick Bentham. Vol 30. No 1. 1972.
The Figure of the House. By John Bott. Royal Shakespeare Company, Stratford-upon-Avon. 1974.

ACKNOWLEDGEMENTS
The author would like to thank Eric Jordan for his meticulously researched drawings of the Old Vic 1871/1880 and 1976; the officers of the GLC in preparing prints of file drawings from which Mr Jordan worked; Miss Molly Sole and the Governors of the Old Vic for loan of photographs; Jason Barnes for advice and loan of a photograph of the Old Vic; Desmond Hall, production manager at Stratford-upon-Avon for loan of photographs and for advice; Miss Connie Dawson and Peter Harlock of the press office of the Royal Shakespeare Company for supplying the most recent photographs; Yorke, Harper & Harvey, architects, of Stratford-upon-Avon for survey drawings used as the basis for the special drawings of 1932 and 1976 drawn by Neville Wood for this article; to the staff of the AR for continuous help during the research period; and to Polonius.

Stephanie Williams
David Hutchinson

The long dream

In 1813 Napoleon was rallying his forces to face the final onslaught of the combined armies of Europe against him before his eventual banishment to Elba; Wellington was fighting his way across Spain. At home, the Tories were in office, income tax was 15 years old and the concept of a National Theatre was born. It is daunting to realise that had cash matched the measure of commitment it might have been George III (or, at least, the Prince Regent) who had performed the opening ceremonies that Queen Elizabeth II presided over in October 1976. The building would have borne a Georgian stamp and not have been on the South Bank of London.

The continuous debate which ensued about what form a National Theatre company should take, let alone that of a building and how it

Geoffrey Whitworth records in his book, *The Making of a National Theatre*,[1] that the collaboration was a happy one: 'Each was the perfect complement to the other. Sir Edwin brought all his genius to the common task, and Masey his talent for inventive adaptability.'

Their compatibility was important and proved by the speed with which they worked. The site was extremely difficult. The brief required an auditorium for 1040 people, a restaurant, theatre offices and storage space. The designs show that a pavilion above a *porte cochère* projecting over Cromwell Gardens would house the offices; the restaurant was at dress-circle level. The entrance hall, with matching staircases rising from either side, suggests a grand but not pretentious space.

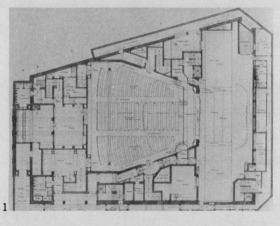 

1, Sir Edwin Lutyens and Cecil Masey's first design for a National Theatre on the still vacant site opposite the Victorian and Albert Museum. The plan shows a single 1040-seat theatre.
2, the South Kensington theatre's elevations are a remarkable example of Lutyens' insistence on symmetry. The balance of fenestration is maintained on all four fronts.

should be funded, carried on for well over 125 years. In the process several sites were considered for the theatre and one in Bloomsbury was actually purchased in 1913 for £50,000. But the rapid rise in building costs that followed the First World War meant that funds could not be found, and the site was sold. It was not until 1937 that George Bernard Shaw received the deeds for that small triangular site that today remains empty opposite the Victoria and Albert Museum, and an architect was first appointed to design a theatre for the nation.

Sir Edwin Lutyens was the first of five men who were to work on the designs for the theatre which Sir Denys Lasdun was eventually to build. He was selected from a list of six 'eminent' architects drawn up by the Shakespeare Memorial National Theatre committee—they had rejected the idea of holding a competition for fear that the ideal design might not result and that the nation's major practising architects might not compete. They persuaded him to give his services free of charge as a public spirited example to inspire contractors and others to donate building materials. Like the others who were interviewed, Lutyens had no personal experience of building a theatre; he was to be aided on the technical side by Cecil Masey, architect of several cinemas.

The honorary secretary of the committee and founder of the British Drama League,

Not a corner of the tiny site was wasted, with dressing rooms and storage space tucked into every conceivable corner between the stage and the auditorium. Externally the elevations were treated with highly disciplined symmetry.

With the completion of Lutyens' model, the appeal for funds was launched, only to be cut short with the outbreak of the war. The theatre committee disbanded its staff, closed down the appeal and the site was offered on loan to the government for the war—put to use housing a fire-fighting reservoir. Lutyens and Masey continued to work on the plans and, writes Whitworth, with a fine turn of astronomical prose: 'Sir Edwin was even turning his attention to the interior decor of the auditorium when suddenly, like a comet in the dark night sky to a meeting of the committee held in March 1942, came Trustee Alderman Blake with a proposition so revolutionary as to change the whole face of the future'.[2]

Blake, as chairman of the London County Council, was, of course, party to the direction of Abercrombie & Forshaw's plans for the future development of London and in particular the South Bank. He suggested that an application for a site for a national theatre in that area 'might not be inopportune' and at the next meeting to discuss the idea it was clear to the theatre committee that the LCC were flirting with the idea of making an offer

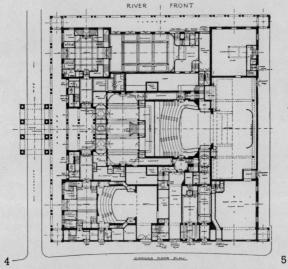

3, plan showing the four South Bank National Theatre sites.

1, Sir Edwyn Lutyens, Sir Hubert Worthington
2, Brian O'Rorke
3, Brian O'Rorke, Denys Lasdun
4, Denys Lasdun

of land on the South Bank in exchange for the South Kensington site. The committee was keen, not only because the South Kensington site was so small, but that it was felt that with the LCC's backing the project would become a reality that much sooner. George Bernard Shaw was a vociferous dissenter and he almost convinced the committee that South Kensington was a better place for a National Theatre.[3] To show everyone what was involved, Lutyens and Masey now set to work to prepare plans for a building that included two theatres on the river front between

Waterloo Bridge and Charing Cross railway bridge. For Lutyens it was to be the last design of his life. The plans went on view at Burlington House early in 1944. They showed a building exactly 250ft square with, once more, a distinctive *porte-cochère*. Arcades ran round the building on two sides; on the entrance front to shelter pit and gallery queues and on the river front to form a terrace on to which the restaurant opened.

But Lutyens died in the same year as the plans went on view. Sir Hubert Worthington, once an assistant in his office, was the next architect to be consulted on the design of the theatre which the LCC suggested should become the centrepiece of commercial and official buildings along the riverside. Worthington's career was impressive: a former Professor of Architecture at the Royal College of Art, architect to Manchester Cathedral, he was responsible for a number of buildings in Oxford including the Radcliffe Library and the library of New College. He had remodelled the old Bodleian and the Radcliffe Camera and built a new boarding house at Eton. His training was in the Classical tradition and his riverside facade for the theatre had all the magnificence of that dying school.

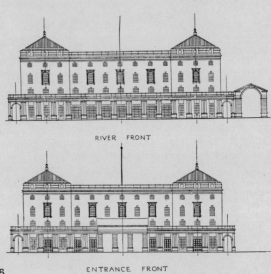

4, Lutyens and Masey's second design for a National Theatre, this time on the South Bank. The 250ft square building contained two theatres.
5, the complete symmetry of Lutyens' Kensington design was repeated in the elevations of this South Bank design.

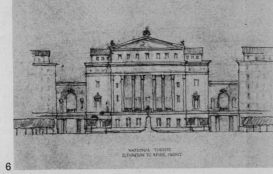

6, second design for the South Bank prepared by Sir Hubert Worthington following the death of Lutyens. It contained two theatres with 1250 and 650 seats.
7, original sketch of theatre standing between Waterloo Bridge and the then proposed Charing Cross road bridge. Flanking terraces return along both road frontages.

But Worthington's career as theatre architect was to be short. He was never officially appointed and the committee was reserved about his scheme. Meanwhile, further changes in the LCC's plans for the South Bank meant moving the theatre site to a larger site next to the future Festival Hall. At the same time, the Shakespeare Memorial National Theatre amalgamated officially with the Old Vic with the aim of jointly building a National Theatre. This combination of events meant that a new architect was needed. In the spring of 1946

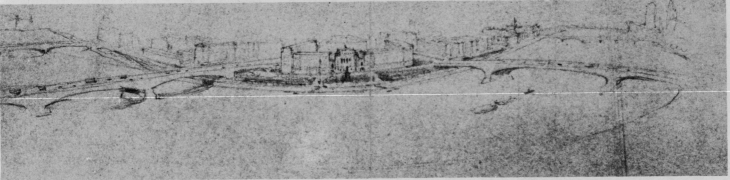

8

8, perspective by Brian O'Rorke showing his first design, prepared in March 1952, for a National Theatre standing on the left of the Royal Festival Hall, next to Waterloo Bridge.
9, O'Rorke's second scheme for the National Theatre, the elevation shows the roof of County Hall in the background.
10, plan of O'Rorke's second scheme. This provided a main proscenium theatre with space set aside within which a second small theatre could be provided when funds became available.

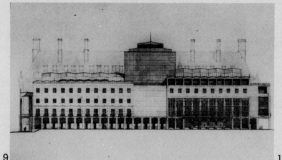

9

10

Patrick Abercrombie, Charles Holden, William Holford, Charles Reilly and Nikolaus Pevsner retired to lunch at the Savoy to select the man. They came out to recommend the appointment of Brian O'Rorke. Although he had worked on the Shakespeare Memorial Theatre at Stratford, the Australian O'Rorke was best known as a designer of the interiors of ships for the Orient Line. He settled down with Cecil Masey to draw up plans for a theatre that was now to have two auditoria (one for 1250 and one for 500) next to the Royal Festival Hall.
All seemed set fair for the project. Legislation was proposed in the Commons to provide not more than £1 million towards the cost of construction provided the LCC gave the building a suitable site. The National Theatre Act was passed in 1949 and in July 1951, during the Festival of Britain, the foundation stone of what had become known as O'Rorke's theatre was laid by the Queen, now the Queen Mother. Publicly, the first delays in getting the theatre under way were blamed on the post-war ban on building for entertainment. But by June 1952 people were beginning to

comment on the theatre's lack of a building permit. In fact, in 1953 it was refused planning permission because of its 'unsatisfactory relationship' to the Festival Hall, and the site moved in the new plans of that year for the South Bank, to a site next to County Hall. The theatre project now entered what must have been the most demoralising period for its perpetrators since the war. Despite the government's agreement in principle on financing and the splendid site on the South Bank, debate was renewed as to whether the theatre was needed at all. If it was, there were many who believed that the South Bank was not the place for it and as for the design itself, surely two auditoria were not necessary?
By 1957 the projected cost had risen to between £1·5 and £2 million and a year later, when an application for outline planning permission for the theatre, on the site next to County Hall was finally lodged, there was still no sign that the Treasury would part with the money promised under the Act, now almost 10 years old. By 1959 it was clear that besides the cost of construction an annual subsidy of £300 000 would be needed to keep the theatre in

11, O'Rorke's perspective of his proscenium theatre.
12, O'Rorke altered his design in 1960 substituting a 1175 seat 'open stage' auditorium for his earlier small theatre.
13, O'Rorke prepared a scheme for a National Theatre and Opera House following the decision of the government to support the project in 1961. He planned his theatre next to Charing Cross Bridge and his Opera House next to County Hall, the opposite arrangement to that later adopted by Lasdun.
14, O'Rorke's sketch of his theatre and Opera House. The theatre was to contain a 1400 seat open-stage theatre on the river front with a proscenium theatre inland. He envisaged the open-stage theatre as half stage and half auditorium within a drum which was exposed on the outside of the building.

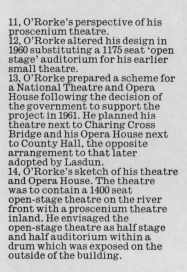

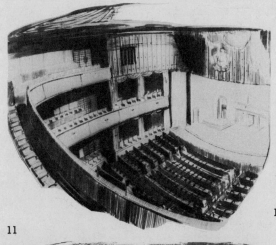

11

12

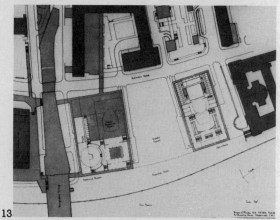

13

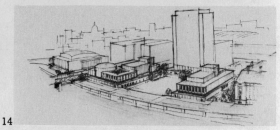

14

15, Sean Kenny's sketches for a national theatre. For him, a national theatre was not a building but a group of excited people. To put up anything that was not entirely experimental was to put up a museum for revivals of past history.
16, Denys Lasdun's design for the National Theatre and Opera House, which filled almost all the space between County Hall and Charing Cross bridge. The National Theatre stood next to County Hall with the small theatre in front of the Shell Centre tower. The removal of the Opera House would have left a site to the left which would have been very difficult to develop.

15

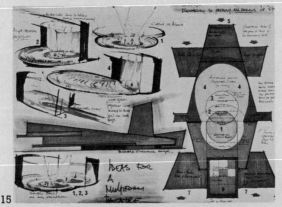

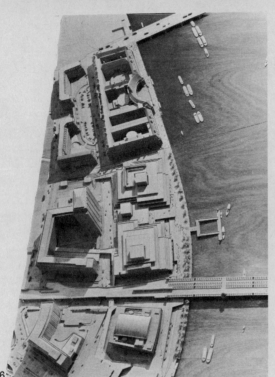

16

[1] *The Making of a National Theatre.* By Geoffrey Whitworth. London 1951.
[2] *Ibid.*
[3] The only dissenting voice was that of George Bernard Shaw. Having originally refused to attend a meeting between the LCC and the Shakespeare Memorial National Theatre Committee, his appearance was something of a surprise. He proceeded to attack the proposed change of site before the bemused National Theatre committee members. He expounded his theory that the West End was moving west, that the Albert Memorial would soon become the cultural mecca of London, and that the right place for a National Theatre was therefore in that vicinity. Shaw circulated his own report of the meeting and eventually the secretary to the committee had to write to the LCC to say that the committee unanimously supported the change. Shaw eventually changed his mind.
[4] This was not the first time that a national theatre and opera house had been proposed for the site between County Hall and Charing Cross Bridge. Harley Granville-Barker had put the idea forward in a book published in 1930 (*The National Theatre*; Sidgwick & Jackson).
[5] People interviewed as possible architects of the National Theatre included James Stirling; Powell & Moya; Philip Johnson; Frederick Gibberd; Gailey & Evans (Eldred Evans); Elidir Davies; Philip Dowson (ARUP Associates) with Sean Kenny; Sir John Burnet, Tait & Lorne; Llewelyn-Davies Weeks Forestier-Walker & Bor; Brian O'Rorke; Peter Moro & Partners.

operation. Nevertheless, that year the scheme O'Rorke had presented was approved in principle by the LCC.

In his second scheme presented in 1960 O'Rorke replaced the small auditorium in his earlier design with an open staged theatre. O'Rorke's design has more the flavour of a large cinema— gangways are wide, the rake of the tiers more gentle and his geometry was based on a circular stage with its centre on the perimeter of the circular auditorium.

O'Rorke's proscenium arched theatre was conventional in the extreme and this, together with the solidity of the elevations gives weight to the reservations held by certain planners in County Hall that the design lacked the kind of lightness and openness that Leslie Martin and Robert Matthew had conceived for the buildings in the area.

In any event, O'Rorke's theatre was not to be. In March 1961 the Chancellor finally announced that the government had decided not to proceed with the project. But he added the proviso that any obligation to build theatres should rest on local authorities and the government would support them with financial help. The LCC, led by Sir Isaac Hayward, then put forward an offer to contribute the estimated £1·3 million needed for the theatre if the government would put up the £1 million it had promised in the National Theatre Act.

When the Chancellor announced his acceptance of this proposal in July 1961 a new element was added: the Sadler's Wells opera company was to join the theatre companies to be housed in the project. One architect was to be appointed for the scheme. Rather than an open competition, the authorities once more favoured inviting a selected list of architects to submit evidence of their ability to design and build a theatre and opera house. There were three architects among the assessors: Sir Robert Matthew, Sir William Holford, and Sir Hubert Bennett, architect to the LCC. John Piper with his knowledge of aesthetics and stage design and Norman Marshall with his technical expertise also sat on the panel.

Among the 20 or so architects invited to appear were Powell & Moya, who turned down the offer to compete because they were simply too busy to take on a project of this scale; and Philip Dowson, with Ove Arup and Sean Kenny, who submitted some sketches. They believed that the theatre should also include a variety of other activities going on in and around it all the time. The firms of Frederick Gibberd & Partners and Llewelyn-Davies, Weeks, Forestier-Walker & Bor were seen, as was Philip Johnson's American practice.[5] Denys Lasdun was selected and his design was unveiled in May 1965. It took up the entire site between County Hall and Charing Cross Bridge, stepping down to a low area in front of the Shell tower. Three auditoria, seating 1100, 750 and 220 and an opera house with 1650 seats were set within a series of terraces.

It was almost immediately apparent that the government was not going to contribute to the building of the opera house or increase its subsidy to Sadler's Wells on a move to the South Bank. The Government's earlier proposal had been based on 1962 requirements for a home base for two opera companies, one serving London, the other touring.

By 1965 the government was considering more schemes for opera houses—which today remain unbuilt—in Manchester, Edinburgh, Glasgow and Cardiff. Where the London opera house had been planned to stand, a vacant site would remain. Fearing for the unbalanced appearance of the sites if the theatre went ahead, the LCC moved the National Theatre to its present site, and Lasdun's final designs got underway.

Colin Amery
Conclusions

The allegory above shows a combination of theatre and circus, as the first line of the poem translated reads: 'The life of man is like a circus or great theatre'. A vast audience is watching from the galleries of a theatre the miseries of the life of man. Alberti's obelisk—the winning post in the race of life, points upwards to the deity beyond the clouds. (Title page from *Theatrum vitae humanae*, by J. J. Boissard; engraved by Theodore De Bry at Metz in 1596.)

It is 25 years since the AR devoted a whole issue to one building. In 1951 it was the Royal Festival Hall which was praised by the AR as 'a modern building—modern in the sense of owing allegiance to no other age but ours—which is also monumental'. Denys Lasdun's National Theatre certainly owes much of its architectural allegiance to our present age but its theatrical roots go back to the Greeks and their theatres. In the same way that the Greeks manipulated their hillsides for theatres, Lasdun has manipulated a piece of cityscape into a building for drama.

Denys Lasdun is a very black and white architect, he does not compromise. His National Theatre is a strong, almost elemental building that glories in the strict geometry of space and in the unrelieved use of raw concrete. From the outside the building appears to be deliberately primitive, a huge lumpen formation that rises from the river bed like a concrete iceberg. To most eyes the abstract and cubist forms of the exterior are still alien, it is a citadel defending some abstract cult that is known and loved only by a small elite. But once the citadel is entered there is an immediate sense of organised space that is comprehensible and moving. The awesome solidity opens up and the public foyers have a sense of dignity and grandeur which elevates them above the mundane nature of their concrete surfaces. There is in this building a sense of some fundamental occasion, a gathering of people to witness some shared ritual. The entrance spaces lead naturally to the heart of the building —the theatres—where the architect's awareness of a basic human love of formal assembly finds its highest expression in the Olivier's arena-like auditorium. Here the architect has done his utmost to heighten the sense of drama, here the life of man is to be played out in an emblematic room. The architect has set the players a hard task, for their words and spectacle will have to resound with the very essence of passion and pity.

It is in the Olivier Theatre that the unadorned abstract forms of the architecture really make most sense; here they suit themes that can be universalised. There is no twentieth-century parallel to the shared popular rituals of ancient Greece; only the football match demonstrates a common shared code of simple beliefs. Polycleitus in 350 BC was building for 14 000 Greeks who all shared the canons of the drama. Lasdun in AD 1976 has had to build for 1160 more diverse souls to indulge a more contrived sense of intellectual community. It will not be the fault of the architecture if the drama does not flourish here.

A visit to the National Theatre is undoubtedly an educational experience for anyone interested in the architecture of the twentieth century. This issue of the AR has looked at the theatre primarily as an important work of architecture. Its heavy investment in technology may be questionable but it is in many ways too soon to judge. But it is not too soon to assess the experience of the building as part of the public realm. By international standards the National Theatre is a cheap building and the success of all the public spaces depends not on expensive finishes but on eloquent, dramatic and heightened expressions of function. Behind the scenes the building is remarkably ordinary, full of expensive equipment but spatially in no way equal to the front of the house.

As a *national* theatre it is a disappointment in the field of patronage; no artists have contributed to the building in any way. This is a sadly missed opportunity—there is no reason why all the visual arts should not have contributed to this home for the art of dramatic performance. The lack of any contributing team of artists perhaps reflects the lack of artistic harmony that often occurs whenever really serious modern architecture happens. It was not always so, architecture in the past was much less doctrinaire and a national building of this calibre would have celebrated more than the rigorous purity of one architectural ethic. Our successors may well be mystified by our enthronement of concrete as a thing of beauty and puzzled by the unrefined nature of so many of the surfaces and the almost total banishment of colour. But they will, like us, delight in the disciplined geometry and space and feel they are in an Acropolis of modern architecture.

Contributors

MARK GIROUARD: Slade Professor of Fine Art, Oxford 1975-76, member of the Royal Fine Art Commission, architectural historian and writer.

WILLIAM CURTIS: writer and art historian at Boston University. Author of books on Le Corbusier for the Open University architecture and design course.

BRIAN BEARDSMORE: architect and interior designer with Dennis Lennon & Partners. His work has included hotels, restaurants, offices, showrooms and domestic interiors.

KENNETH ROWELL: Australian-born stage designer and painter who has worked for many of the leading English theatre companies. His work includes designs for opera, ballet and dramatic stage productions. He has written and lectured on theatre design and his paintings are to be found in many public and private collections.

RICHARD PILBROW: producer and theatre consultant. Chairman of Theatre Projects Group and a director of Light Ltd. He is theatre consultant to the National Theatre. He has produced a number of plays and musicals.

IAIN MACKINTOSH: theatre designer and historian and a director of Theatre Projects Consultants. He is a director of Prospect Theatre. He has been involved in the design of the Eden Court Theatre, Inverness, and the Cottesloe Theatre at the National Theatre and is currently advising on the renovation of the auditorium and stage at the Theatre Royal, Nottingham.

STEPHANIE WILLIAMS: architectural journalist.

DAVID HUTCHINSON: architect, town planner with the GLC.

Acknowledgments

COVER and FRONTISPIECE pp2-3: Richard Einzig. COSMIC CONNECTIONS p4: Tim Street-Porter. Pp9, 10, 12, 13 (top), 24, 28, Donald Mill; p11 (bottom), Eric de Maré; p13 (bottom), Sam Lambert; p22, Martin Charles; pp27 (top), 30 (bottom), Andrew Berg; pp27 (bottom), 29, John Donat.

DETAILING THE DRAMA pp31-35: 2-17, Andrew Berg; 18, Richard Einzig.

OLIVIER THEATRE pp36-39: Richard Einzig.

LYTTELTON AND COTTESLOE THEATRES pp40-42: p40 (top), Donald Mill; remainder Richard Einzig.

SCENIC POTENTIAL pp43-44: 3, 4, Robert Kirkman; 5, 7, Nobby Clark; 6, *The Guardian*.

INNOVATIONS p50: Rackhams of Lichfield.

PERSPECTIVE pp52-58: 4, 16, Behr; 6, John Donat, 9, *Eastern Daily Press*; 10, 11, 14, Richard Einzig; 18, 30, Toomey Arphot; 24, Dell & Wainwright; 25, Hedrich-Blessing; 26, Peter Carter; 27, T. O'Brien; 28, Henry A. Wood; 29, 38, Cervin Robinson; 33, André Martin; 36, Charles Correa; 37, G. E. Kidder Smith; 39, Wolf Lücking; 40, Martin Charles.

'SCENE INDIVIDABLE OR POEM UNLIMITED' pp59-64: 1, Crown copyright; 4, Millar & Harris; 5, Angus McBean; 7, Toomey Arphot; 9, 10, Walter Scott; 11, Joe Cocks; 13, Shakespeare Centre Library. Drawings, Old Vic, Eric Jordan: Stratford, Neville Wood.

THE LONG DREAM pp65-68: 1, 2, 4, 5, Butler *Country Life*; 8-14, RIBA; 15, *Sunday Times*.

PORTRAITS: p15: Zoë Dominic; p25 and p45: Anthony Crickmay; p48: Godfrey Argent.

The AR gratefully acknowledges generous contributions towards the cost of colour printing from: Crown House Engineering Ltd; Theatre Projects Consultants Ltd; Concord International Lighting Ltd; Hille International Ltd.